BY FLARE OF
NORTHERN LIGHTS

Boo

ROTHERHAM LIBRARY & INFORMATION SERVICE

Russell ~~1 0 JUL 2014~~	Beevers Stocks	
Linton Rochester 1 3 NOV 2014	1 4 JUL 2015 Knowles	
~~Hayter~~ ~~1 6 JAN 2015~~ 1 6 JAN 2015	2 5 JAN 2016 Whittingham 2 5 JAN 2019	
Walker ⒺⒷ 1 3 FEB 2019		

BY FLARE
OF
NORTHERN LIGHTS

TIM CHAMPLIN

SAGEBRUSH
Large Print Westerns

Copyright © Tim Champlin, 2001

First published in Great Britain by ISIS Publishing Ltd.
First published in the United States by Five Star

Published in Large Print 2014 by ISIS Publishing Ltd.,
7 Centremead, Osney Mead, Oxford OX2 0ES
by arrangement with
Golden West Literary Agency

CIP data is available for this title from the British Library

ISBN 978–0–7531–5352–9 (pb)

Printed and bound in Great Britain by
T. J. International Ltd., Padstow, Cornwall

For my granddaughter
Ruby Elizabeth Champlin

Oh it was wild and weird and wan
and ever in camp o' nights
We would watch and watch the silver dance
of the mystic Northern Lights.
And soft they danced from the Polar sky
and swept in primrose haze;
And swift they pranced with their silver feet,
and pierced with a blinding blaze.
They danced a cotillion in the sky;
they were rose and silver shod;
It was not good for the eyes of man —
'twas a sight for the eyes of God.
It made us mad and strange and sad,
and the gold whereof we dreamed
Was all forgot, and our only thought
was of the lights that gleamed.

from *The Ballad of the Northern Lights*
Robert Service

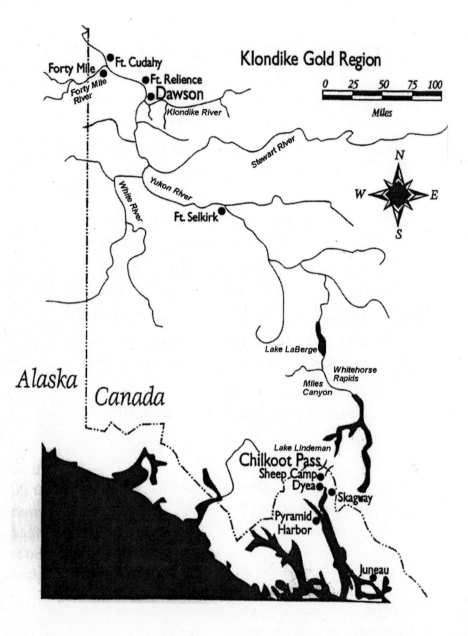

Klondike Gold Region

Forty Mile • Ft. Cudahy
Forty Mile River
• Ft. Relience
Dawson •
Klondike River

0 25 50 75 100
Miles

Stewart River

White River

Yukon River

Ft. Selkirk •

N
W   E
S

Lake LaBerge

Whitehorse Rapids

Miles Canyon

Alaska | Canada

Lake Lindeman

Chilkoot Pass
Sheep Camp •
Dyea •
• Skagway

Pyramid Harbor •

Juneau

Prologue

Gold! We leapt from our benches.
Gold! We sprang from our stools.
Gold! We wheeled in the furrow,
fired with the faith of fools.
Fearless, unfound, unfitted,
far from the night and the cold,
Heard we the clarion summons,
followed the masterlure — Gold!
Robert Service

When the steamer, *Excelsior*, tied up at the San Francisco docks on July 14, 1897, it discharged a cargo that was destined to set the nation ablaze like nothing had done since the War Between the States. Several dozen rough, bearded miners, fresh from the creeks of Alaska and Canada, staggered down the gangway with bags and pokes of all sizes, loaded down with dust and nuggets that amounted to more than a ton of gold.

Three days later, while the shock of the *Excelsior*'s arrival was still vibrating California and the telegraph wires, the steamer, *Portland*, nosed into a berth at a Seattle wharf, and an additional sixty-eight sourdoughs from the North waddled ashore, lugging nearly two tons of the precious yellow metal. There was no secret about what these men were carrying; they had found

1

their fortunes and were vocal about proclaiming that fact to the world at large.

Before the day was out, newsboys on the streets of Seattle were hawking copies of the *Post Intelligencer* whose banner headline screamed — **GOLD! GOLD! GOLD!** — in crimson letters two inches high. The following Sunday's issue of the *Chicago Tribune* ran a story that "Gold in Seattle is weighed by the hundred pounds. The *Portland* is here from the Klondike with treasure weighing more than a ton." The catch phrase, "a ton of gold," staggered the imagination of most people who tried, usually in vain, to imagine how much of a pile or a stack that would make. In actuality, later calculations showed the weight to be closer to two tons. It was reported that a John Wilkerson stepped ashore with nuggets worth $50,000, Dick McNulty with $20,000, Frank Keller with $35,000, Frank Phiscator with $96,000, and even an eighteen-year-old boy with $3,000. And these amounts were figured at the current exchange rate of $16 per ounce.

This came at a time when the country was in the fourth year of the lingering 1893 financial panic (an economic condition later termed a recession). Banks were failing, and Coxey's army of unemployed had marched on Washington in 1894 as hard times spread from coast to coast. Heavy gold exports had depleted the national treasury, while the West was advocating the silver standard.

Restless men and women who were lamenting the closing of the Western frontier suddenly had hope once again for a chance to seek their fortunes in a new wild country. Those who were picking over the leavings of earlier gold fields at Angel's Camp, Tombstone, Creede, and Cripple Creek packed their rock hammers, pans, and shovels and headed north. But not only the die-hard prospectors were lured. The news that hit the country like an exploding mortar shell blasted loose even the most sedentary of settled citizens. Stable boys, barbers, butchers, milkmen, policemen, cowboys, judges, factory workers, clerks were drawn like June bugs to the glow of the golden lamp. The Alaska canneries were deserted; university football players abandoned their summer jobs and took the first boats north.

It was quickly evident that this Northern wilderness did not boast the benign California climate that had greeted the '49ers a half century earlier. At least some preparation was required to survive in the forests and mountains of the Far North — a land that reportedly lay in ice-bound darkness several months of the year.

Newspapers, stores, and travel bureaus shortly began posting lists of essential supplies that each person needed to take: flour, 500 pounds, dried fruits, and evaporated potatoes, 200 pounds, dried beans, bacon, rice, tea, coffee, and salt to a total of 2,000 pounds. One ton of supplies was estimated to last one man one year. In fact, there was a rumor abroad that the Canadian government was not allowing any prospector across their border into the Northwest Territories without enough food to last a year. Besides the food, each man would have to take a tent, shovel, gold pan, boots, woolen socks, and plenty of warm clothing, axe,

3

saw, matches, and hundreds of other smaller items that were considered the basic necessities. The old sourdoughs who had returned with their fortunes related that the interior of the Yukon could be reached by boat along a string of lakes which fed into the Lewis River (called the Yukon below Fort Selkirk). It was this river and the creeks that drained into it that had washed down the several tons of gold they had taken out. Maps were drawn up and professionally printed, detailing the various routes, as thousands of dissatisfied and adventurous people scrambled to put together a stake.

Those who had property quickly put it on the market to raise money for an outfit. Pages of want ads in the newspapers across the country ran such notices as: **For Sale — will sell my ranch for a stake to Alaska. Make me an offer. For Sale — fine saloon in excellent neighborhood. Excellent paying trade. Cheap. Owner leaving for the Klondike**.

Others, who had enough money, merely closed their businesses and put a sign on the door that they had gone to join the gold rush. Thousands who rushed north became known as stampeders, or Argonauts, and the sudden fever that gripped them caused many to mortgage their homes and stores to pay for passage, sleds, woolen union suits, picks, dogs, and grub. If a man had nothing to sell and no cash, he could sign on with a party or syndicate, agreeing to divide any gold he found, ever confident there would be plenty left over for him.

Port cities such as Seattle boomed overnight. Hotels were crammed to overflowing with people from every state and several foreign countries. As the demand for sea passage shot up, fares on such steamers as the *Portland* leaped skyward from $200 to $1,000. Instead of waiting until August for her return trip to Alaska, she was rescheduled to return in five days following her arrival. When she pulled out July 23rd, she was loaded with 125 passengers, and 1,000 tons of freight, mules, dogs, and burros. On the same day, the *Queen* sailed with 250 passengers and full load of freight. Then followed the *City of Topeka*, the *City of Mexico*, and the *Topeka*.

The *Umatilla* then arrived in Seattle, bearing another load of miners and gold to fan the fires of Klondike fever. She made a quick turnaround in twenty-four hours and headed back north crammed with 400 passengers. The *Victoria* sailed, loaded to the gunwales, while the *City of Seattle* was being remodeled to carry three times her normal quota. On July 29th, when the *Excelsior* left San Francisco, 10,000 curious people including an unknown number who couldn't crowd aboard jammed the dock to see her off.

Old ships from all over the world converged on the West Coast ports of Canada and the United States to cash in on the boom. Even the *Ning Show*, a Chinese freighter, steamed across the Pacific fitted with rough lumber bunks four tiers high in her hold. She loaded up and left for Alaska with nearly 1,000 passengers, plus horses, mules, and dogs aboard. Prices were high while food and traveling conditions were poor to terrible. But

5

most of the stampeders ignored these hardships. They could put up with anything for a few days until they could reach the coast of Alaska. For just beyond the coastal mountains lay the coarse gold that only waited to be scooped from the gravel of the creeks and rivers. In light of that, what were a few temporary inconveniences along the way, when wealth and luxury beyond imagining lay at the end of their trek?

CHAPTER
ONE

"Farewell!" we cried to our dearests;
little we cared for their tears.
"Farewell!" we cried to the humdrum
and the yoke of the hireling years . . . ;
The spectral shores flitted past us,
and every whirl of the screw
Hurled us nearer to fortune,
and ever we planned what we'd do —
Do with gold when we got it —
big, shiny nuggets like plums,
There in the sand of the river,
gouging it out with our thumbs.

Robert Service

Desperation! It stung Terence Brandon like a silent lash and had driven him to throw over his job, leave his fiancée, and bolt for the Klondike. His stomach knotted in fear of the unknown as he watched the cargo boom lift and swing the long gangway aboard the *Ohio Belle*. A deep-throated blast on the steam whistle overhead signaled their departure, and three black roustabouts ashore threw the bow and stern hawsers off the cleats, effectively cutting his lifeline to the past.

As the riverboat's bow swung away from the pier, he suddenly longed to go back and resume his old, comfortable ways. No irrevocable commitment had yet

7

been made to the hardships of the Far North. Even now he could still get off the boat at one of the downriver stops and return to Louisville. He could even ride out his ticket as far as St. Louis, and it wouldn't be too late to abort the trip. But he couldn't return. Jobs were hard to find, and he'd abruptly quit his clerk's position with no notice. His friends had thrown him a farewell party at O'Brien's saloon, and afterward he'd wrenched himself away from a tearful Nellie Gentry, his co-worker and fiancée. For better or for worse, he was committed at least *to try*. He'd gone this far, and pride would not let him cave in just as he was starting.

He gripped the rail and swallowed hard. His stomach was queasy. Too many beers and too little sleep, he told himself. It wasn't just his uneasiness at plunging into this mad rush to the Yukon. For several perilous seconds he felt as if he were going to vomit. He took several deep breaths, and the sensation gradually passed, leaving him weak and sweat-drenched under his light cotton shirt. He looked quickly up and down the deck to see if any passengers were observing, but no one was within fifty feet of him as the sternwheeler continued swinging across the current to point its jackstaff downstream.

He considered lying down to rest in his stateroom, but the stifling July heat in the tiny room would make him feel even worse. He sucked in great lungfuls of the fresh, relatively cooler air blowing across the wide expanse of water. Letting go the rail, he made his way aft to watch the huge paddle wheel churning up a white

8

wake. Trees were rapidly hiding the low-lying buildings of Louisville behind them.

His stomach was still uneasy as he mopped his damp face with a shirt sleeve. The jerky motion of the boat didn't help. Instead of sliding smoothly through the water, the *Ohio Belle* was being thrust forward with a pulsing throb that was transferred up through his body from the deck. As the big paddle wheel revolved, each row of paddles slapped the water in turn, shoving the boat ahead with a continuous series of steady beats.

He ignored the thumping surge of the boat and took a firmer grip on his emotions, trying to view more dispassionately the reasons for his leaving. At age thirty-three, his life seemed to be flowing past him faster than the water alongside this boat. Only two weeks ago, he'd noticed the first traces of gray in his thick brown hair. If he were ever going to make something of himself, it was time to get at it. Engaged to be married to one of his co-workers at the Life of Louisville Insurance Company office — what a ridiculous notion! He could never support a wife on the salary of a dead-end clerk's job. The two of them, and any future children, would be in poverty for years to come and probably dependent on the charity of relatives. He shuddered at the thought. Better to make a clean break now and gamble on something greater. If he failed, at least he was no worse off. If Nellie wouldn't wait for him, then it just wasn't meant to be.

In retrospect, he viewed his twenties as a lost decade. Floundering from job to job, he'd filled the void of a purposeless existence with laughter and alcohol. His main problem was a lack of any strong interests or talents. In spite of constant effort, he couldn't find a job that was worthy of his heart and soul. A job he did only for pay was merely half-done drudgery. For several years he'd tortured himself with the hope that somewhere out there was a vocation to which he could dedicate a lifetime of enthusiasm, and from which he could gain satisfaction as well as a livelihood. He envied scientists, teachers, priests, and others whose vocations were also their avocations. How could anyone be passionate about selling paint or working in a factory or clerking in an office? It was only a way of trading one's life, hour by hour, for bread and a roof. The dream of a job he could love was rapidly slipping away. This trek was just a last, frantic grab for wealth that would allow him the leisure to pursue whatever interested him. But, deep down, he knew it was a very long shot.

"No such luck for me," he muttered aloud to himself. "I'm old enough to know better! Running away to find a fortune!" he gritted between clenched teeth.

"What did you say?"

Startled, he looked up into the soft eyes of a woman standing at the stern rail a few feet to his left. She was dressed all in white and carried a small white parasol to shield her face and black hair from the sun.

"Sorry, ma'am. I was just thinking out loud." He could feel his face reddening, and hoped it blended with his healthy tan.

"Oh." She turned to look at the sweep of the river behind them. "Lovely, isn't it?"

10

He nodded, then realized she was not looking at him. "It sure is. I never tire of it."

"You spend a lot of time on the river?"

"Not on riverboats. I usually rent a twenty-foot sloop on weekends and do some sailing." The thought of a picnic on one of the river's wooded islands with Nellie and his friends already made him homesick

The woman in white favored him with a coquettish smile as she spun the parasol on her shoulder. Then she looked out over the red paddle wheel, flashing wet in the sun as it churned up a continuous, fine mist.

"Steamboats are becoming a thing of the past," she said. "But I do love them. A cruise is so relaxing, don't you think?"

"Very much," he agreed. "This boat only runs three times a week now, and carries more freight than passengers. Are you going far?"

"Oh, yes," she replied, favoring him with another sidelong look. "George and I are on our way to the Klondike."

He was jarred. "Really? Wouldn't the train be a lot faster?" The incongruity of his own method of transportation occurred to him. Perhaps he'd taken the slower *Ohio Belle* because he didn't really want to go to the gold fields himself. And just now the *Belle* was nosing into the canal that would take it safely around the series of rapids known as the Falls of the Ohio River.

"We started from Cincinnati. This just seemed the easiest way to travel until we get to the other side of the Mississippi. We'll be cooped up in a train long enough."

He started to ask who George was, but refrained. This woman was only a casual acquaintance, and he felt no need to pursue anything personal. He didn't even feel obliged to tell her he was also bound for Alaska.

They stood in silence for a minute or two, enjoying the passing scenery. He was actually beginning to feel a little better. A whiff of cooking food from the galley even made his stomach growl. The sun was almost overhead; it was time to eat.

"I'm hungry," she said, as if reading his thoughts.

"I was about to suggest some lunch," he said. "May I join you? I don't know anyone else on board."

"Perhaps we should introduce ourselves, then," she said with a smile. "I'm Annie O'Connell." She extended a slim hand.

"Terry Brandon," he replied, taking her soft grip. He couldn't imagine this woman in the Northern wilderness. She could have just stepped out of a fashion ad in *Harper's Weekly*. The ruffled front of the high-necked, long-sleeved shirtwaist accentuated, rather than concealed, the thrust of her breasts. Even though she was a petite woman, probably not over thirty, he wondered if the tiny waist was corseted to remain that size. The long skirt swept the deck as she turned to accompany him toward the dining salon.

He could feel the soreness in his back and shoulder muscles as he held a chair for her at the long, narrow table inside where about a dozen other passengers had already gathered. A favorite way of working off frustrations involved bruising games of sandlot football played on weekends with several of his athletic younger friends. Any future soreness would be due more to hard work than hard play, he thought, as he seated himself beside her.

"That's another reason I love to travel by steamboat," she said as he handed her a bowl of mashed potatoes. "The food."

Stewards were setting down platters of steaming Brussels sprouts and sweet potatoes, sliced turkey breast, gravy, and dressing. The aroma piqued his appetite.

"The owners probably figure this is the best way to hang onto their passengers," he replied, helping himself to some fresh sliced tomatoes. "Some of those dining cars and trackside eateries leave a lot to be desired."

"Fred Harvey's places are pretty good," she said. "But the train stops only thirty minutes, so you have to gobble down your food."

Conversation lapsed for a few minutes as they turned their attention to the food. The clinking of glassware and the low murmur of voices were the only sounds as white-jacketed Negro stewards ghosted in and out with hot coffee and fresh bread.

The motion of the boat brought a languid breeze from the open doors forward. But Brandon was perspiring freely in the muggy heat. Being careful of his still-unsettled stomach, he ate only small portions of three vegetables and some turkey. Passing up the dessert, he finished off with a cup of hot coffee. Almost immediately, the food began to restore his flagging spirits and energy.

"So, where are you bound, Mister Brandon?" Annie asked, helping herself to a brandied peach.

He was reluctant to discuss himself, but said: "The Yukon."

"Oh, my!" Her eyes widened, and she paused, spoon poised in mid-air. "Then we're going in the same direction." She took a bite and chewed daintily. "I wonder how many of the passengers at this table are stampeders?" She looked down the long table at the twenty other passengers, young and old, men and women, who shared the dining salon.

Brandon shrugged. "All the younger men are going to the gold fields. Most people my age have the sense to stay home and tend to business," he added, thinking of Thad Bowman and Johnny Crews, two of his best friends. Thad had a comfortable job as a court clerk, and Johnny worked in his family's hardware store. They'd both declined offers to accompany him.

"People your age?" Delicate brows arched as she scrutinized him. "Lord knows, you're probably all of twenty-eight," she declared. "Men and women of *all* ages are going to the Klondike. It isn't only young men. Why, my George is nearly sixty!"

Brandon nodded, wondering what had possessed this unlikely couple to join the stampede. But, from the way she was dressed, he judged they probably had the money to outfit themselves and pay the inflated fares. His own pockets contained $390 — his entire worldly savings after he'd bought his steamboat ticket. To outfit himself would cost at least $200–$300. Then there was train fare to the coast and passage from Tacoma or

14

Seattle. He had no idea how he would even *reach* the gold fields.

"Huh? Sorry. I was distracted," he mumbled, suddenly aware that she had asked him a question.

"Are you meeting a party out West?"

"No." He had a sudden desire to confide in someone. "To tell you the truth, I'm going at this alone and just trusting to luck and opportunity to see me through."

"We're going to Alaska to get some gold," she said airily. "But George thought maybe we shouldn't go alone, so he attached us to a syndicate. We're to meet them in Chicago, then take the train to the coast. Maybe you could join us," she suggested brightly, as if referring to an afternoon picnic. "My, how can you drink that hot coffee on a day like this?" she pattered on before he could answer. "The weather is so awfully hot. It just made George sick, and he had to lie down in our stateroom."

"George?" he finally asked.

"My husband. He hasn't been well lately. That's why he left his law practice in Cincinnati. He thought this trip would be a good getaway for his health. He'd been wanting to travel a bit."

"You're going all the way to the Yukon? That might be hard on a sick man," Brandon ventured, not wanting to get too personal, although this woman was talking to him as if they were long-time acquaintances. Or was she one of those scatter-brained women who never had a serious thought, and whatever entered her head popped right out of her mouth?

"He'll be all right directly," she answered, a slight shadow crossing her features as she looked away. "I still think it would be wonderful if you could join us."

"I'm pretty much of a loner," he said, thinking that he certainly didn't want to saddle himself with this fashion plate, her elderly husband, and a bunch of city-soft businessmen. He was reasonably young and fit and — short of money. Maybe he'd be wise to reconsider her offer. But, no, it was too early to be looking for lifelines. Besides, she was only making polite conversation.

He looked at her profile over the rim of his coffee cup, but his mind was on Nellie Gentry. He was surprised how much this Annie O'Connell resembled her in size, coloring — even hair style. What was Nellie doing now? Probably at her desk in that sweltering office where he'd also spent the last year and a half. He shuddered at the thought of the confinement he'd escaped.

"Do you have any family, Mister Brandon?"

He winced at the formality. "I'll call you Annie if you call me Terry."

"Terry it is."

"My parents are still living. Two married sisters and a five-year-old nephew." He decided Nellie should not be paraded out for further query.

"I'm always curious about people," she said, dabbing her lips with a linen napkin. "I guess I'm asking what prompted you to go to the Klondike."

He would be candid, but vague: "After I read the news of the gold strikes, it took me exactly five days to make up my mind I needed a change and a chance to better myself." He smiled. "Nothing new in that. I expect most people . . ."

The crash of breaking crockery interrupted. He shot a look toward the forward end of the salon where a disheveled man had staggered into a steward who was bearing a tray of dishes. The man reeled drunkenly, gray hair falling in his face as he scanned the passengers at table. He was hardly fifteen feet from them.

"George!" Annie gasped.

"Ann, my love," he articulated with the care of a drunken man trying to retain control. "You failed to waken me for luncheon."

"I couldn't wake you up," she muttered in a cowed undertone.

Brandon glanced at her face that had gone suddenly waxen.

"Ah, I see. You've lured another handsome young man into your web!"

"George, sit down!" she said, beginning to recover. "You're making a scene."

The table had gone silent, and all heads were turned in their direction.

"By God, I'm about fed up with your spending my money and taking lovers behind my back!" he thundered, lurching toward them, grabbing at the back of a chair to steady himself.

Brandon slid back from the table and tensed for an attack. Annie's face had gone from pale to a rosy pink.

"So this is your latest?" He leaned forward to peer at Brandon. "Doesn't look like anything special to me. Were you two going back to his stateroom after lunch?"

Brandon was frozen, not knowing how to react to this onslaught.

"Why don't I just puncture his hide and see if that doesn't cool him down a little." A Derringer suddenly appeared in George O'Connell's hand.

Brandon was halfway to the floor when the little pistol jetted flame. The blast slammed his ears, and he heard Annie scream as he rolled under the table. Yelling. Chairs scraping. The thump of bodies falling. Crashing glass. He scuttled to one side and got to a knee. Two of the crew and a passenger had George O'Connell pinned across one end of the table. Gravy spattered his white shirt.

"I think the captain will want to see you," the purser said as the three men hustled their captive out the forward door of the salon.

Giving Brandon an anguished glance, Annie hurried after them. The rest of the passengers gradually settled back into their chairs, talking quietly to each other and casting curious glances in Brandon's direction.

"That was a close call," a big man nearby said, pointing a meaty finger at a splintered spot on the door casing behind him where the lead slug had struck.

"Damn," Brandon muttered under his breath. Was this an indication of what this trip was going to be like?

CHAPTER
TWO

**Bid good-by to sweetheart, bid good-by to friend;
The Lone Trail, the Lone Trail follow to the end.**
Robert Service

An hour later Terry Brandon was summoned by the purser to the captain's cabin where he was questioned about the incident.

Captain Atchley, a gray, weathered relic of a river man, was nearing the end of his career, the purser confided. But this fact had not softened the captain's rigid discipline aboard his vessel. After a few terse questions, Captain Atchley apparently satisfied himself that Brandon was an innocent party in the matter and dismissed him. Terry found a deck chair on the shady side of the boat and spent the next two hours watching the green, wooded shoreline glide by as he pondered the violent episode. Then his thoughts turned ahead as he tried to figure a way to finance the rest of his trip.

Just before suppertime that evening, the boat nosed into the pier at Owensboro, Kentucky. From the rail of the hurricane deck Brandon watched the roustabouts load sacks of coal for the boilers. He was suddenly shocked to see Annie and George O'Connell struggling down the gangway, helped with their considerable luggage by two Negro porters. Either they'd had a falling out and were aborting their trip, or the captain had decided he needed no more of George O'Connell and had them put ashore. Brandon couldn't make out their words, but their strident voices carried up to him as they snapped at each other.

When they stood among the leather grips and hatboxes on the wharf, George yelled for a hotel hack, but there was none nearby.

"Damned one-horse town!" he fumed. "Where's a hack? Is there a hotel in this burg?"

The roustabouts ignored him as they came and went, offloading some freight and carrying aboard cordwood and gunny sacks of coal. While her husband ranted and stormed for assistance with their dunnage, Annie seated herself on a steamer trunk and looked up at the boat. Brandon caught her wandering gaze. From this distance he wasn't sure, but she appeared to have a tearful, appealing look. He suddenly felt sorry for her, but knew there was nothing he could do. Captain Atchley could have had her husband arrested for assault or attempted murder. But the captain was of the old school. It was much simpler to put the man off than to drag the law and its complications into it. If someone had been killed or wounded, it would have been a different matter.

Less than an hour later, a blast on the steam whistle signaled their departure, and the gangway was swung aboard. The sun was casting long shadows across the river as the sternwheeler backed away from the pier and resumed its downstream journey. The O'Connells were still sitting on their luggage when Brandon turned away toward the salon.

The rest of the trip to St. Louis was relatively uneventful. Brandon spent most of his waking hours lounging about the deck, watching the scenery. Safely beyond the reach of the crazy George O'Connell, he slept well and ate well. He knew nothing of the other passengers, and, given what had occurred when he'd struck up a casual conversation with Annie O'Connell, a total stranger, he was shy of even passing the time of day with any of the others. For their part, they mostly eyed him curiously, as if trying to determine if he were the guilty party in some clandestine love affair that had outraged a jealous husband. He felt their stares and guessed what they were thinking. A time or two as he ate alone in the salon, he was tempted to jump up and shout his innocence to one and all. Of course, any such action would only confirm the fact that he was guilty or crazy, or both. Shutting the other passengers out of his mind, he went about his business of killing time, letting them think what they would.

An afternoon thunderstorm swept down on them just as they entered the Mississippi and turned north. The *Ohio Belle* slowed somewhat, but plowed straight ahead, bucking the current in the middle of the river. The pilot was just feeling his way, Brandon thought, as he clung to a stanchion under the shelter of the hurricane deck and watched the gray veil of rain hissing down, blurring visibility beyond fifty yards. Since passenger steamers no longer plied the river on a regular basis, there was little danger of colliding with a downward-bound boat. But coal and grain barges might be a threat. Smaller vessels would just have to look out for themselves. He hoped the pilot knew the shoals and islands, since the rain had made this like navigating in a fog.

He moved back out of the wind-blown spray and propped himself in a deck chair in a dry spot. Lightning flashed through the murk, followed by booming thunder that rattled the ironwork. He loved the excitement of a wild thunderstorm, especially one that cooled the steamy heat, but the other passengers had sought shelter inside, leaving him the only person on the wind-swept deck. Alone with the elements, he wondered if this is what solitude would be like in the Far North. He expected hordes of people in Seattle, and even though he couldn't envision the vastness of the Yukon wilderness, he still pictured the rivers and settlements as crowded with thousands of newly arrived gold-seekers from the States.

The storm slowly eased off to the northeast, and, by evening, the setting sun was lancing shafts of light under the lingering pall of clouds. The boat followed the twists and turns of the great river on into the dusk. An hour later the moon rose, flooding the broad river with a silver reflection.

Brandon didn't go to bed early that night. He sat alone in a deck chair near the port bow, listening to the bow wave swishing alongside the boat as he sipped a glass of wine and watched the moon's ghostly light shimmering on the wide expanse of water. It was the last night of such serenity. Tomorrow they would reach

St. Louis, and he would begin the hectic train trip to Chicago and Seattle. He wished there were some way he could travel all the way to the coast by river steamer.

At home he would have been at a saloon with his friends, oblivious to the night sky. Or, he would have been asleep in his boarding house, enclosed by the walls. He had never really camped or lived in the outdoors for any length of time. Could he adapt to an outdoor life in a wilderness? Certainly he was more capable than many of those flocking north. But that didn't mean he would be successful. If he could somehow sustain himself, he might be able to strike gold. But were all the good places already claimed? He knew little of geology. Would any of the experienced old-timers share their secrets and advice with him? It would take several more weeks to reach the gold fields, and there was no need to worry about things he couldn't control until he got there and saw what the situation was. This brought him back to the problem of not having enough money to outfit himself with the proper gear. Then, he would have to pay someone to haul part of it; it would be impossible for one man to haul over a thousand pounds without much back-tripping. He instinctively felt freer and faster traveling light, but a certain amount of food, clothing, and camping gear was essential to survival. This could not be a solo effort. He would probably have to ally himself with others. As much as he disliked the idea, he might be forced to throw in his lot with strangers. Changes could be made later, if necessary.

He drained the last of the sweet sherry and took a lingering look at the moon and the liquid silver of the vast river before rising and heading for bed. They would arrive in St. Louis about noon the next day. A good night's sleep always made his prospects look cheerier.

Even though an outfit could be purchased cheaper inland, Brandon had decided to travel with only one leather grip until he reached the coast. The reasons were twofold — his continued ambivalence about making the trek at all, and the trouble and expense of hiring porters and stevedores to carry all his gear from boat to hotel to train and back again.

As it was, the railroad ticket he bought in St. Louis routed him via Chicago and St. Paul through to Seattle. Following a night in a second-class downtown St. Louis hotel, he walked to the depot and boarded a coach for Chicago. Settling into his seat, he pulled out his billfold and surreptitiously counted his remaining greenbacks. He had barely over two hundred dollars remaining. The cost of food in the dining car was prohibitive, and he resolved to eat as little as possible. For the rest of the way to Chicago he sustained himself with several cups of the train's excellent coffee. During a four-hour layover at Union Station, he walked to the nearest eatery and filled up on a greasy steak and vegetables. At a general mercantile he bought a small back pack and from a corner grocery filled it with bread, sharp cheese, two bunches of grapes, three apples, and some sticks of smoked beef.

24

Thus fortified, he returned to the huge, cavernous depot and at 4:40p.m. boarded the train for St. Paul. He had no money for a Pullman berth, but that didn't bother him. He was young and could nap in his seat. During the night at St. Paul, he changed to a tourist car on the Great Northern. The next morning he awoke somewhat stiff, but rested, to gaze out on the sparkling lakes and forests of Minnesota.

By the time they were on the treeless high plains of North Dakota, his misgivings about starting on the trip had nearly vanished. At least, as time and distance passed, these thoughts were less frequent.

At rural stations, teen-age boys offered the passengers freshly killed wild ducks at the bargain price of twenty-five cents a pair. Brandon and several others were quick to lay in a supply. For a share of the food, the porter roasted them, and Brandon, as hungry as he was, had never tasted anything better. He licked the grease off his fingers and had a cup of coffee, hot from the stove at the end of the coach.

Eating, chatting with a few of the passengers, and dozing, he passed two days of the journey across the waving wheat fields and rangelands of North Dakota and Montana. Then the train began laboring up the switchbacks of the Rocky Mountains. The scenery was spectacular, and Brandon could not get enough of it, hating to see night coming on and darkness hiding the magnificence. He wondered if the mountain ranges of Alaska were as huge and intimidating as these snowcapped peaks and dizzying gorges.

On July 28th the Great Northern train ground to a halt at the Seattle depot in a cloud of hissing steam. A block from the station he secured a room at the Commercial Hotel. After checking in, he dumped his back pack and grip and went out into the street. From all appearances, the town was jammed with Argonauts of every size, shape, and background. He wandered up and down, window shopping and pricing flour, beans, oatmeal, rice, cornmeal, bacon, sugar, canned meats, and evaporated fruits. He totaled the figures roughly in his head, adding cooking utensils, a Mackinaw, woolen union suits and socks, gloves, boots, hatchet. He didn't even consider pick and shovel, pan, crosscut saw, or rifle. The rifle was the only thing he thought might be in short supply up North. His friends had given him a new, single-action .38 caliber Colt Bisley model revolver with a six-inch barrel. This would be good for defensive purposes, but impractical as a weapon for hunting meat.

A real shock came when he elbowed his way through the crowds into the ticket office of the Pacific Coast Steamship Line. Before he got to the barred ticket cages, he heard snatches of loud conversations above the crowd noise that told him what he didn't want to hear, but he squeezed up to the window anyway and asked the harried clerk: "How much for a one-way ticket to Alaska?"

"I've got berths left on the *Umatilla* leaving September Eighth," the clerk replied. He pulled off his green eye shade and wiped the sleeve of his striped shirt across his sweating brow.

"September!" Brandon was stunned. "How much?"

"Going for nine-hundred each right now."

"Nine-hundred!"

"You heard me right. If you wait, they'll be gone, or the price will go up," the clerk said, turning his attention to another man who had shoved in beside Brandon, waving a sheaf of greenbacks.

In a daze, Brandon wormed his way back through the milling crowd to the outside door. He had expected to find hordes of people and inflated prices, but had not anticipated there would be no berths available for more than a month.

When he reached the street, a low overcast had settled in and the sea breeze was blowing in a light mist. Accustomed to the heat and humidity of the Ohio Valley, he felt almost chilly. He tugged down his hat brim and walked aimlessly down the street. Was this where he was destined to abort this trip, thwarted by lack of money and unavailability of transportation? He gritted his teeth. Surely he could be more resourceful!

He found a small grassy park with several large trees and took shelter under one of them. From his shirt pocket he pulled a list he had compiled on the train — a list of supplies he considered indispensable. No need to purchase them now, if he couldn't get passage until September. Maybe he should get a train south to San Francisco, or north to Vancouver. But he felt sure the ticket situation would be just as desperate in those places, and, as expensive as an outfit would be here, it would likely be impossible to get or pay for if he waited until Juneau or Skagway.

He shoved the list back into his pocket and decided to do a little shopping. Couldn't hurt to see what affordable items he might pick up to carry in a pack. He was still obsessed with the idea of traveling light. But this was like going on an expedition to the Sahara: one man could not pack everything he would need. Even if he could get a ship, how could he, as one man alone, hope to succeed? Logistically it seemed impossible. But he should have thought out all this before he left Louisville.

He sighed and started up the street, looking in the store windows. He was on the point of eating the last of the dried food he'd hoarded in his pack, when he saw a menu in the window of a Japanese restaurant. He thought the sign was probably a come-on and found it hard to believe all that was listed for a price of fifteen cents. But he went inside. And for that ridiculously cheap price he was served clam chowder, salmon with onion, and a slice of lemon, boiled potatoes, radishes, corncake, bread and butter, and tea. He wondered how they would ever make a profit, but didn't question his good fortune.

The streets were lined with businesses catering to the stampeders, he noted. These merchants would make plenty of money from the gold rush without even leaving home. Everything was on prominent display in the windows and along the sidewalks out front. Heavy woolen shirts, denim pants, gold pans, parkas, snowshoes, skis, canvas packs, shovels, picks, and something he at first took to be a small, wooden washing machine with a vertical handle for the manual agitator. He paused to study it, then realized it was some sort of device that resembled drawings he'd seen of a crude gold separator. Inside the window of the general mercantile were sacks of flour and beans, and signs advertising, for a stiff price, dried fruits of all kinds. Sides of cured bacon hung on hooks, alongside fur caps and gloves. It was a sellers' market. Everything necessary for a Northern trek was here — for a price.

Above the clutter in the display window, a beautiful Marlin carbine caught his eye. Gleaming blue-black barrel and receiver, a polished walnut stock, it would make a good hunting rifle that wouldn't be too large or heavy to carry. A price tag hung from the trigger guard. Maybe he could trade in his revolver on it. But no, the pistol was a going-away present from his friends, and he couldn't part with it.

The door was propped open to admit some fresh air and, he supposed, to allow the owner to watch his sidewalk display. Brandon stepped aside to let three men pass before going in. He reached up to lift the rifle off its peg by the small of the stock. At the same instant, another hand gripped the barrel. Startled, he turned and found himself staring into a man's face not two feet away.

CHAPTER
THREE

Let us probe the silent places,
let us seek what luck betide us;
Let us journey to a lonely land I know.
There's a whisper on the night-wind,
there's a star agleam to guide us,
And the Wild is calling, calling . . . let us go.
Robert Service

"Sorry. Go ahead." The man let go of the barrel, the flat planes of his face relaxing into a smile. His white, even teeth were interrupted by one of gleaming gold. Thick black hair was combed straight back, the edges reaching his white, open-collared shirt. He sported a new leather vest.

Brandon lifted the Marlin down and turned it over to get hold of the dangling price tag. The other man looked on.

"Whew! A hundred ten." Brandon hefted the rifle, noting its balance. It was not overly heavy. He swung the curved brass butt plate to his shoulder. The weapon was an extension of his arm, with a pointing finger. "Nice. But too rich for me," he added reluctantly.

"May I?" the young man inquired politely, holding out his hand.

Brandon handed over the carbine, and watched as the other worked the lever and examined the design and features. "Marlins aren't nearly as plentiful as Winchesters," he remarked, sighting along the barrel. "But I believe I like the design a little better."

Brandon said nothing, not being familiar with the nuances of difference between the two makes.

The man looked closely at the stamping on the octagonal barrel. "This one's a Forty-Four. Plenty powerful for deer or moose." He nodded in satisfaction. "Lucky I found it," he said, swinging the weapon into the crook of his arm as he reached for a billfold in his hip pocket. Then he paused. "Oh, but you got here first."

"No. I can't afford it." Brandon was embarrassed. "It's all yours."

"Obliged. You headed for the gold fields like everyone else in town?"

"Yeah." Brandon nodded as the two of them walked toward the long counter. This man, who looked to be in his late twenties, moved with the grace of an athlete, but had the pallor of an office worker. The vest, white shirt, and tan canvas pants tucked into his boots were all obviously new.

Brandon pretended to examine a woolen Mackinaw as the young man paid for the Marlin. If everyone around here had as much money as this man, Brandon wondered why any of them were going to look for gold.

"Milton Conrad's the name." The young man thrust out a hand. Brandon took it, estimating the man's strength by his grip. Conrad seemed open and genuine. "Terry Brandon. Where you from?"

"Baltimore." He spat out the word as if it were distasteful. Then his face brightened. "Have to get moving. See you on the trail." Holding the rifle at his side, he pushed his way through the crowd and disappeared out the door.

Brandon left the store and spent the next hour wandering in and out of shops along the streets, noting prices, gauging his remaining capital, trying to figure out what to buy. He wound up purchasing a large pack and frame, then selected some woolen socks of German manufacture he'd been told were the best, two flannel shirts, a heavy parka with fur-trimmed hood, high-topped trail shoes with cleated rubber soles, a box of ammunition for his .38 Bisley, two sets of woolen long underwear, fur-lined mittens, a block of sulphur matches in a waterproof container, a frying pan, a hatchet, tin cup, fork, knife, spoon, three bars of soap, and, as an afterthought, a tiny sewing kit, along with some bandages and a bottle of alcohol. He already had a small Kodak with several rolls of film, a leather-backed journal, and supply of pencils to record this trip. Without buying food or rifle, he kept his stake to only what he could afford and carry. His remaining cash amounted to $187.25 — $140 in bills and the rest in gold and silver coins.

Now would come the hard part. He slipped his arms through the pack straps and went out into the street, thinking he would return to the hotel, gather his few belongings, and check out.

32

The steamer, *Queen*, was scheduled to sail that afternoon. He plunged into the noisy crowd gathering near the wharf and began shouting to make himself heard. "How much for a ticket on the *Queen?* Who wants to sell their passage?" After several minutes of this, he began hearing other men doing the same thing. It sounded almost like some crazy auction, but those with tickets were not selling.

Finally, a man in a rain-soaked derby answered: "You can take my ticket for twelve-hundred."

"You're out of your mind. That's robbery."

"Take it or leave it." The man spat in the street.

Brandon shook his head and moved off toward the water-front. Ten minutes later he had worked out on the other side of the throng, and he knew his quest was hopeless. The few available tickets were bringing scalper's prices — at least five times what he had in his pocket. But now, rather than being discouraged, he was stubbornly determined.

He returned to the Commercial Hotel, packed his personal items, and checked out. Somehow he would gain passage, even if he had to stow away and sleep on deck, hungry all the way. Nothing would deter him. If he had to stop here in Seattle and work for a stake, he might as well go home; instinctively he knew that to hesitate would be to lose out to winter and the competition. The challenge to his ingenuity set him on edge. Gone were any thoughts of returning home. If he had to steal a ticket, he would. He justified this thought by reasoning that it was not stealing to take a ticket

33

from someone who was willing to rob some fellow traveler of $1,200 for it.

At first he'd been appalled by the shoving, shouting, cursing mob of humanity, and wanted to retreat from it. But, as he drifted along the edge of the seething throng near the waterfront, a slow, unexpected change came over him. It was a feeling of wounded pride at being pushed aside, a gradual gathering of strength and confidence. His was not an aggressive nature until pressured or stung to the point of fighting back. And he now realized that, beginning on this Seattle dock, he would have to fight his way to the Yukon.

It was nearly time for the ship to get underway, and Brandon shouldered his pack and waded into the churning sea of humanity crowding the pier. Strident voices were raised in last-second buying and selling; couples were saying their last good byes.

A sudden commotion drew his attention. Someone's Jersey bull was objecting to being loaded aboard. He bucked and jumped and scattered the spectators, even though there was hardly room for them to move. While the bull was glaring belligerently around, three men quickly slipped the wide canvas sling under him and hooked it to the overhead cable. Before the bull realized it, his hoofs were hoisted clear of the dock. Bellowing, he was swung aboard to the cheers of the crowd.

Brandon had one desperate ploy in mind. If that didn't work, he'd try something else. There would be other ships. He elbowed his way to the gate in the iron fence that had been erected across the pier head. The pilot gave a long, deep-throated blast on the steam whistle to signal departure. While the roar of the steam whistle was drowning every other sound, Brandon silently signaled the gatekeeper to open up. The gate swung inward, and Brandon stepped through. The gate slammed and latched behind him. The uniformed guard held out his hand for a ticket.

Brandon shoved a wad of bills — all he had left — into the man's hand and started quickly up the gangway. His heart was pounding. He suddenly felt a vise-like grip on his arm.

"Your ticket!" the guard shouted, then lowered his voice as the steam whistle abruptly stopped. "I can't take money. You have to have a ticket." He shoved the roll of bills into Brandon's side pocket.

"That was just a tip," Brandon said, pulling his arm free. "I'm bunking with a friend. He's got my ticket . . . in his luggage."

"Don't give me any of that, mister. I've heard 'em all. No ticket, no boarding." The burly man kept a hard grip on Brandon's arm. "If I could take cash, half that crowd out there would be on this vessel . . . and I'd be a rich man. But this steamer is loaded to capacity now." The man was not belligerent, but Brandon suspected he could get that way if provoked. He had the size and grim visage of a saloon bouncer.

"But, I've got a friend who has . . . ," Brandon protested.

"Yeah, and I know the president of this shipping company, but you're still not going aboard without a ticket." He dragged Brandon back toward the gate. The clamor on the pier was deafening, and the guard had to shout to make himself heard. The roustabouts were heaving off the stern spring lines.

"Hold it! That man's with me!" a voice shouted. Brandon felt the gangway vibrate under the weight of several heavy steps. He turned to see Milton Conrad.

"Don't matter. He has to have a ticket." The guard was adamant as he opened the gate.

"Here's his ticket, right here!" Conrad cried above the noise. He held out two tickets. "Mine and his."

The guard let go of Brandon and inspected the two slips of cardboard, only one of which bore the holes of the guard's punch. He looked dubiously at Conrad and Brandon, as if suspicious of being swindled, but couldn't quite figure how. "OK, go ahead," he finally said, perforating the ticket with his punch and handing both back to Conrad.

Brandon was bewildered as well, but grateful, and followed his benefactor up the stage. The cargo boom began to lift the gangway from the pier.

The main deck was jammed with those fortunate enough to get aboard who were waving to their friends ashore. Brandon followed Conrad as he bored through the throng and then inside to a starboard passageway. They stopped at a door amidships and entered a small cabin with a two-tiered bunk along one bulkhead.

"You're on top," Conrad said, raking a pile of packages and bags off the upper bunk onto the floor. "I don't like heights . . . especially in any rough seas."

Brandon shrugged out of his pack and heaved it into the head-high bed. "I don't know what to say . . ." He pulled the roll of bills from his pocket once more and held them out. "Here. This won't cover the going price, but it's all I have."

Conrad gave him an easy smile, flashing the gold tooth. "Put your money away. You'll probably need it later . . . for some o' this." His arm swept around at his supplies.

For the first time, Brandon was aware of the clutter in the tiny cabin — sacks and boxes of food, a pair of snowshoes, even a two-man crosscut saw sticking up from the pile that took up most of the floor space. The Marlin carbine lay on the lower bunk atop some folded clothing.

"You can pay me back by packing some of my gear when we hit the beach in Alaska."

"How come you happened to have two tickets?" Brandon asked.

"I wanted some extra space for my gear so it wouldn't be stowed in the hold where it could get pilfered. Besides, I'm particular who I bunk with."

"You don't know *me*," Brandon said.

"Not yet." Conrad pulled a flat, silver case from his pocket and selected a cigarette. "But I will soon enough. We met this morning. And I don't have to know a man long to size up his character." He struck a sulphur match on the door frame and lit his cigarette. A cloud of smoke billowed out into the confined space. "If we decide we can't stand each other by the time we get to Alaska, you can help me ashore with my stuff, and we'll call it even and go our separate ways."

Brandon nodded, still somewhat stunned. He half expected some official or ship's officer to burst in and order him off the overcrowded vessel, regardless of the ticket. Then he felt the measured throbbing of the engines through the steel deck and heard a great cheer go up from the assembly on the pier as the ship began to back away. If he was to be put off, the ship would have to return to its slip, and the crew would have to go to a lot of extra trouble. Not likely they'd bother just to put one man ashore. His breath whistled out in a sigh of relief at his good fortune. So what if the ship was probably dangerously overloaded? The absentee owners would reap the profits, not take the risks. This was a voyage up the inside passage with few stops. Even if he never reached the gold fields, he was at least assured of getting to Alaska — the first giant step in his quest.

The food, included in the price of the ticket, was surprisingly good. Breakfast at seven in the morning, lunch at half past eleven, and supper at four-thirty. Generally the fare consisted of beef, veal, stew, soup, beans, oatmeal, potatoes, coffee and tea, bread, biscuits, and butter.

That evening at supper, Brandon found out considerably more about his benefactor. Milton Conrad was actually Milton Conrad IV.

"The Fourth?" Brandon echoed. "There are three more of you?"

Conrad winced. "I've long since dropped that appellation," he said. "And that's one reason I'm here."

Brandon sipped his hot tea and waited for the other to continue.

"My name means nothing to you?"

"Sorry. Can't say that it does."

Conrad gave him a look of relief. "Don't be sorry. I'm glad you never heard of me. Let's just say I stand to inherit a considerable fortune through a company my great-grandfather started and my grandfather and father have expanded. As a fourth-generation eldest son, it was my misfortune to be in line to shoulder the load my family will drop on me very soon."

"Carrying a fortune is a load? I'm sure some of those old Alaskan sourdoughs who struck it rich don't think so."

"Well, everything comes with a price tag. If I could just sit back and collect the money, it would be fine. Unfortunately at the age of thirty . . . next year . . . I'll become the chairman of the board of Conrad and Sons, which means taking on all the responsibilities and headaches that go with that position. It means major business decisions, involving millions of dollars, fighting with members of a board who are old-line conservatives, making decisions that could affect the jobs of thousands of workers and their families, even the future of the company, becoming involved in several charitable trusts, altruistic civic projects. In other words, life in a fishbowl."

"Hmm. In your case, it seems a high price to pay for fortune."

"Exactly."

"Conrad and Sons . . . is that the same company that has been manufacturing steam engines for years?"

"Correct. This ship is probably being powered by our engines right now. But steam power is on its way out. With the advent of electricity, I'm supposed to guide the company into the new century. The board is recommending that we branch out into manufacturing trolley cars, as the use of steam declines. It will require at least two new plants, an outlay of millions, some of which we'll have to borrow, and all kinds of head-splitting decisions that are designed to shorten a man's life and cause sleepless nights and gray hair." A morose look came over his face, and he pushed back from the table, leaving the rest of his supper.

"Never thought of it that way," Brandon said.

"I did. I do. Every day. That's why I'm here now. I don't need the gold. I came to get away. I'm awfully tempted to just keep going and lose myself in the North, maybe fake my death."

"Can't you abdicate or something? Don't you have a younger brother who wants the job?"

"My brother Delbert is four years younger and would love it. He's got a real head for business, too."

"Then what's the problem?"

"Two things. If I refuse to accept my rightful responsibility, I disgrace myself and the family. And, secondly, if I don't assume this job as the fourth Milton Conrad, I inherit only a pittance when I turn thirty next year. I'd have to go out and earn a living on my own. And all I've ever known is the family business. For seven years I've been given jobs in different aspects of the operation to train me in what is being done and how to do it. After all this training, my father would never allow me to completely quit. I'd be an outcast . . . thrown on the slag heap with no inheritance."

"Surely your own family wouldn't do that to you."

"How little you understand of families with power and money. Any sign of humanity is looked upon as a sign of weakness." His mouth set in a grim line.

A poor rich boy, Brandon thought. *And I've been feeling sorry for myself for not being able to find a vocation.* This man had a vocation already planned for him before he was born, and all the riches he could ever dream of, yet here he was dreading his future straitened existence.

"If I'm forced to work outside Conrad and Sons, I also have to support my wife and baby son." He forced a sickly grin. "So now you know I'm running *from* something, instead of *toward* something," he concluded. "At least, I had plenty of money to outfit myself. I've never taken orders from anyone but my father in my life. So I couldn't align myself with one of those parties of stampeders, even one whose leader had experience at this sort of thing."

"You can't be serious that all your family's money has made you completely unhappy," Brandon ventured, refusing to believe, literally, what he'd just heard.

"Oh, of course, it's not *all* drudgery," he replied. "I have my own yacht to sail with my friends on the Chesapeake. And I've become a pretty good polo player." He gestured at the gold front tooth. "Souvenir of a match. A constant reminder that I never should've put a mallet in the hand of a drunk and allowed him to play, even if he *was* a friend. Polo playing and yachting on the Chesapeake, garden parties, drawing-room conversation, the latest fashions . . . all very predictable

41

and very boring when you travel in the same circles all the time."

"Your father agreed to your going?"

"Oh, hell no! But he doesn't run my life."

"He was afraid of the danger?"

"I'm not sure that was it. He looks at me not as a son but as a well-groomed company asset that he can't afford to lose. He wants to retire and travel next year. I can just see that . . . I'll be getting cablegrams every week from Europe or the Greek Isles *suggesting* I do this or that. He won't let go of the puppet strings, and I'll have to act like they're my decisions. Actually" — he paused reflectively — "since I have a yen for adventure, he would rather I accept a commission in the military as long as there is no war going on. It's the glory, you understand . . . the uniform and the contacts with dignitaries, and all that. If the Army actually had to fight, I'm sure I'd be given a safe job behind the lines and out of harm's way. Wearing a uniform in peacetime is infinitely preferable in social circles to falling down a crevasse in some glacier or being eaten by a bear in the faraway Klondike among the rabble." There was a bitter edge to his voice.

Better to let him talk out his frustrations to a stranger, Brandon thought. "You grew up in Baltimore?"

"From the time I was ten. Before that, Pittsburgh."

"What kind of city is Pittsburgh?" Brandon asked, trying to lead him away from the subject of his inheritance.

"Dirty. Smoky. That's why my father moved the company headquarters to Baltimore. We certainly wouldn't want to breathe the same congested air that our foundry workers are breathing," he finished with a twist of sarcasm.

"What did your wife think of your taking off?"

"She wasn't crazy about the idea. Couldn't really understand when I tried to explain why I had to go. I was choking in that rarified atmosphere. Judith is a society girl, but level-headed and practical. She's from a good family in Connecticut. Huh! . . . listen to me." He shook his head, a sneer on his face. "There I go again, talking about family connections and wealth. Ingrained habit, I'm afraid. But Judith is a great girl. Fine wife so far." He paused to take a bite of biscuit. "I miss her already. Leaving her behind is my only regret. But she couldn't go with the baby, and would never leave him with a nanny."

He mentioned no money considerations. But, for a man of his means, it was nothing that need concern him.

The *Queen* reached Victoria, British Columbia during the night and docked for three hours. Next came Union, B.C. where the steamer took on coal. Even though it was long past midnight, Brandon was awakened by the docking of the ship. He got up in the dark, slipped on his pants and shirt and shoes. Then he realized Conrad was not in his bunk. He went out on deck where he found his benefactor leaning on the rail, smoking a cigarette. The engines slowly turned, pushing the ship into the night, and the lights of the coaling station faded into the darkness.

"So you couldn't sleep, either?" Conrad greeted him.

"The motion of the ship and the racket up here woke me. I had to get some air."

"You mean all that noise in there?" He jerked his head toward the salon.

For the first time, Brandon was aware of the sounds of a party in full swing. "What's going on?"

"They've been partying like that since the sun went down. Damnedest thing I ever saw," he went on. "You'd think they were on a permanent picnic."

From inside the spacious main cabin came the thump of a champagne cork popping, punctuated by a cheer from the crowd.

"Oh, honey, my glass is empty!" a feminine voice shrilled.

"Leave some for me," a man answered.

Then the conversations were drowned by the sounds of music as the band struck up.

"Get up there! That's it . . . on the table where we can see!" someone shouted.

There was cheering and clapping.

A hulking figure loomed up near them in the darkness and paused at the rail as the man raked a match to life and touched it to his pipe. The flare of light revealed a bearded face with craggy nose and deep-set blue eyes. He blew out the match, and the aromatic smoke drifted over to Brandon.

"Do you reckon we shipped half the dregs of Seattle?" Brandon wondered aloud.

"Hardly," Conrad replied. "There're lawyers and doctors and teachers aboard. I heard 'em talking

44

earlier. Most of those people aren't the scum of society."

"Huh!" The big man near them grunted in the darkness. "Then they got more dollars than sense." He spat over the side. "Damned Cheechakos! They won't pan out three men to the boatload!" he growled in a deep voice.

Brandon took this man for an old-timer returning to his diggings. The three men fell silent for several seconds. The sounds of revelry grew behind them. The steamer was rocksteady as it sliced through the calm sea. Brandon took a deep breath of the fresh air. Overhead, a million of points of light twinkled in the moonless night sky. The faint mark of a white foam bow wave slid past the iron side of the vessel.

"This ship is really moving," Conrad remarked. "I hope the helmsman or the officer of the watch is sober. There's not much discipline among the crew. They've joined in the carousing. Since we left Seattle, the purser and the first officer have been drunker than two barn owls."

"They could sure as hell pile this tub up on the rocks, if they ain't careful," opined the bearded passenger. "I been up and down this inside passage a few times. It's considerable calmer than the ocean, but it ain't all that safe from hazards."

The old sourdough, who introduced himself as Bob Saunderson, proved to be a prophet two days later. The ship passed through Queen Charlotte Strait, leaving Vancouver Island behind, and was threading its way along a narrow passage between the mainland and a chain of islands. Terry Brandon and Milton Conrad stood on deck, their warm jackets warding off the chill sea breeze, and watched the rocky shores slide past. The steep slopes, heavily forested in fir and spruce, slanted to the water's edge.

Just after ten o'clock, a fog began to roll in and quickly grew heavier, blurring the nearby shoreline. The dark evergreen forest seemed to swirl away and disappear into the thick mist.

"Eerie," Brandon remarked.

"Feels like we're standing still," Conrad said.

The engines slowed, but the ship still made headway, feeling its way through the murk, the human eyes in the pilothouse guiding it. Brandon's stomach tensed. There was no way the helmsman could see where they were going. He looked at Conrad whose face expressed the same thought.

The big sourdough, Saunderson, came on deck just then, cutting a chew from a plug of dark tobacco with his jackknife. His blue eyes squinted in the white glare, then settled on the two of them. "Damn," he breathed, working the cud into his cheek. "Like a white-out. But I'd take a good snowstorm to this any day."

The fog thickened and swirled around the three men on deck, obscuring the dim shapes of other passengers who had stepped outside. A jangle of bells suddenly sounded from the wheelhouse, then a muffled shout and a sharp command. The vibrating engines died, and Brandon held his breath in the several seconds of silence that followed.

Suddenly the ship jerked. Metal screeched against rock as the hull bumped something, then drifted free. A chill went up Brandon's back. He saw black granite boulders slide past, and dark spruce trees passed within yards of the ship. His heart pounded heavily in his chest. The ship was on the rocks!

CHAPTER
FOUR

Oh, they shook us off and shipped us o'er the foam,
To the larger lands that lure a man to roam;
And we took the chance they gave
Of a far and foreign grave,
And we bade good-by forevermore to home.
Robert Service

The long, scraping noise finally ground into silence as the ship stopped. Brandon stole a quick glance at the sourdough. The big man was gripping the rail, spitting the remains of his chew overside. His face above the blond beard was pasty white in the misty light. "Mary's Island," he muttered. "Near got us last time, too."

Brandon wondered if the hull had been holed by the rocks, but knew, if the ship started to sink, they'd have a chance to escape over the rail and wade through the boulders to the island. An eerie stillness pervaded for two or three long minutes while the engines were shut down. Then the faint jangle of bells from the bridge signaled the engine room, and the slow throb of the steam engines began, swinging the stern of the *Queen* away from the obstruction and out into deeper water. Brandon let out a long breath as the engines were given half-ahead, and the ship once again began to move cautiously forward.

Several minutes later a rift appeared in the fog ahead. Welcome shafts of morning sunlight lanced through the shredding tendrils of mist. The shoreline of Mary's Island became visible, and the ship bore to starboard around the point where several men on shore seemed to await their arrival.

"Customs," Saunderson said. Wiping the dampness from his face with a big bandanna, he turned to go inside.

The American officials made a quick inspection of the captain's papers, then the ship moved on to the next stop. It was a place the map identified as Gravina Point, where Saunderson, now recovered from his nervousness, pointed out a salmon cannery.

As the ship proceeded north that day, they marveled at the magnificent scenery. Snow-capped peaks were visible miles away in the clear air. Forests that had never seen the lumberman's axe marched up the slopes to timberline beneath jagged, upthrust rocks. Mature, white-headed bald eagles soared over the tiny inlets, watching for fish. Sleek porpoises leaped alongside the ship. Now and then, in the middle distance, the gray back of a whale broke the surface of the glittering sea. It was a wild, elemental country they were entering. Brandon and Conrad couldn't get enough of it, sitting in deck chairs for hours, breathing the cold fresh air and drinking in the grandeur.

They arrived at Fort Wrangell an hour before midnight. The ship docked for the night. The sky was still not completely dark, and most of the passengers went ashore to stretch their legs. In spite of several churches and an Indian mission, the place bore a primitive look. Frame buildings, their roofs covered with moss, stretched along the base of a mountain that was swallowed in a chill mist. Saloons and gambling houses were going full blast, filled with a mixture of whites and Indians. Dogs roamed the muddy streets while Oriental-looking Haida Indians sat on their doorsteps and peddled home-made wares — snowshoes, horn ladles, moccasins, and caps. Carved totem poles seemed to grow from the ground. They passed a sawmill that apparently was the source of the boards for the frame buildings, and just on the other side of the mill was a brewery where the noisy party crowd from the ship had gravitated. The saloon that fronted the brewery sold beer for twenty-five cents a quart and was doing all the business they could handle.

Brandon and Conrad each bought a quart. As they walked outside, they ran into Saunderson. With a sigh of contentment, he wiped the foam from his blond mustache. "Gets mighty dry on that ocean," he remarked when he looked up and saw them.

"You headed back to the ship?" Conrad asked.

Saunderson nodded. "Need something to keep me wet down till I get there." He joined them. "Good fur market here," he said. "Maurice Chofsky used to be the principal dealer. Some of the old-time trappers still peddle their furs here. It's closer than 'most anywhere else . . . except for the Hudson Bay trading posts. But there ain't no dealing with that company. They got their set prices, and that's it. You ain't gonna get the better of them." He paused for a hearty draft of his quart. "I'll be a spavined mule if this gold boom don't kick the bottom outta the fur market," he added. "Rooshians started this place years ago as a fort afore the Americans bought Alaska. I disremember what they called it then."

Even though summer daylight came early, the ship didn't get underway until noon. Two hours later they were steaming through a place Saunderson identified as the Narrows, bucking the tide, and winding around islands and between hidden rocks, carefully keeping to a buoy-marked channel. The protected waters were alive with ducks. Great chunks of ice calved from the face of LaConte Glacier had cascaded into the ocean. In spite of the amount of drifting ice, the sun was still hot on their faces, warming the air around them. Brandon and Conrad spent most of the afternoon sorting and packing his gear into gunny sacks, bundles, and boxes, and still there was more than even Conrad had anticipated. "I had somebody else helping me buy this outfit," he remarked, eyeing the pile on the cabin floor as they paused to take a breather just before supper. "Maybe I can buy a couple of pack mules when we get ashore."

"Saunderson said there were some horses available last time he was up this way, but he didn't remember seeing any mules."

"I'm just glad we didn't tie ourselves down with a bunch of cattle. Seems like one or another of them have been bellowing down in the hold since we left Seattle."

"Well, they may be a bother to travel with, but at least those people will be assured of having plenty of meat," Brandon said. "Or they'll sell and trade them for something else."

The ship steamed up the long inlet called the Lynn Canal, by-passing the turnoff to the village of Skagway. Saunderson pointed out Haines Mission on the port side. He was relaxed and grinning as if he'd been too long away and was almost home.

In the lingering twilight they finally reached the raw settlement of Dyea at the head of the inlet. The *Queen* let go one of her anchors and came to rest a half mile off the beach. Brandon wondered why they had anchored so far out from the little town at the foot of the mountain. Then he noticed the tide was out, exposing several hundred yards of mud flats leading up to the beach. The stench of rotting fish and mold came to his nostrils. He could not imagine a less inviting landing place.

"Maybe we should have landed in Skagway," he remarked, eyeing the dreary sight.

"The map shows this as the beginning of the shortest trail to the mountains," Conrad said. "Saunderson told me there's a long pier at Skagway, but a steamer with the draft of the *Queen* can't land alongside. Still have to use lighters."

Before the ship had fairly settled into her anchorage, the decks were aswim with passengers, all trying to be the first off. Passengers and goods would have to be lightered to the gradually sloping mud flats. Scows pushed alongside, manned by both whites and Indians from the village.

"I've marked all my stuff with an **MC**. Should be easy enough to keep track of," Conrad said, raising his voice to be heard above the clamor on all sides. He slipped the Marlin carbine over his back by means of a makeshift rope sling.

The purser approached with a harried look on his face. Brandon grabbed him by the arm. "Can you get someone to give us a hand with this?"

"Not now!" He jerked away and kept going.

"It's up to us," Conrad said. "Catch hold and let's get this out on deck."

By the time everything was piled near the starboard rail, boxes and bales of all shapes and sizes were being swung overside and handed down to the waiting scows. Every ship's officer and deckhand was being besieged by at least a dozen shoving, shouting passengers, all intent on being the first ashore.

"You'd think those mud flats was sprinkled with gold dust," Bob Saunderson marveled, watching the commotion. "I reckon that's why they call 'em stampeders. They'll get calmed down soon enough." He looked at the two men. "Looks like you're gonna need an extra pair o' hands with all that." Apparently his low opinion of Cheechakos didn't extend to them.

"You don't have any gear of your own?" Conrad asked.

"Not so's you could notice," the big man answered with a grin. "I long ago learned to travel light and make do. You'll get the gist of it if you stay here long enough. Besides, my stuff is all at my claim downriver."

Cargo doors in the side of the ship gaped open, and the donkey engine screeched, belts slipping on pulleys, as outfits and cattle were hoisted from the hold.

"Back 'er! Back 'er!" came a shout, and Brandon looked up just as the corner of a big wooden scow crushed the side of a poling boat, knocking two of its three occupants into the water.

"You damned lubbers! Where'd you learn to row?" a red-faced man shouted. He clung to the stern to save himself from being pitched over. He was answered with a string of curses from the four rough-looking men manning the scow. The red-faced man awkwardly swung a paddle at them, lost his balance, and took a header over the side to join his companions, thrashing around in the cold water.

A half dozen brawny Indians lounging at the paddles of a forty-foot canoe laughed at the sight of the fracas, but most of the *Queen*'s passengers ignored the dispute, intent on their own problems. While Brandon was watching this scene, Saunderson grabbed one of the deckhands and shoved a pack into his hands, then yanked two other passengers back from one of the ship's launches. "This 'un's already taken!" he said, shoving them aside. They took one look at the bearded giant and decided not to argue.

The four men quickly threw the sacks and boxes of food and gear into the boat, even as two of the crew were swinging it overside on its davits. The boat was lowered into the water, and the falls unhooked. The twenty-foot boat barely held all their supplies, but they had to shove the pile fore and aft to make room for two men at the oars. The crewman and Conrad pulled strongly toward the beach, leaving the turmoil of debarking passengers behind them.

The boat grounded in the soft mud a long way from the village.

"Shit!" Conrad said, eyeing the black ooze between the boat and the beach.

"Reckon we should wait for high tide?" Brandon asked.

"No time," the crewman said. "I've gotta get this boat back for another load. The captain made it plain he wants to be off before the tide turns in two hours."

"Let's get at it, then."

Back-tripping through the knee-deep muck with heavy loads was exhausting work. Perspiration ran down their faces and soaked their shirts. Hands occupied, they couldn't brush away the biting flies and mosquitoes, swarming around their heads. Brandon was glad for the high, lace-up boots he wore; shoes would have been sucked off in the stinking mud.

Passengers toiling shoreward from the *Queen* and another steamer anchored nearby formed a steady line of human ants that carried packs and bundles nearly as large as themselves back and forth from beach to scows. They churned through the black goo, bent over, two and three men to a crate.

As Brandon returned for a final load, he saw the crewman dump the last of their sacks into the mud and shove off, rowing away.

"You damned slug!" Saunderson roared. "Come back here and I'll bust your head!" He looked at the soaked and muddy sacks. "Throwin' the flour in the mud!" He shook his head as he rescued a fifty-pound bag and heaved it onto his shoulder.

"Now I wish I hadn't slipped him that five-dollar tip," Conrad muttered. He scraped the clinging mud from his pack and flung it down, wiping his hands on his shirt.

"Maybe we should have landed at Skagway," Brandon said.

"Not unless you're going up the White Pass," Saunderson replied. "Anybody with cattle and horses will have to go that way because the pass is longer and more gradual. Chilkoot's 'way too steep for livestock. Damned near too steep for men." He squatted and threw a fifty-pound sack of beans on the other shoulder, and slogged away toward the beach. "Besides," he said over his shoulder, "the mud's about as deep and wide there."

After spending hours studying the map aboard ship, Brandon had memorized it and now pictured it in his mind. Dyea was at the very head of the inlet at the mouth of the Dyea River. It was the beginning of the Chilkoot Pass Trail, while Skagway, around a point of land a few miles to the south and west, was the beginning of the White Trail Pass. In both cases, the mountain chain had to be crossed to reach the interior. The White Pass Trail was longer — maybe eighteen to twenty miles — and reputedly rough, but not extremely steep. The Chilkoot Pass Trail was shorter by about

56

half, but the last part of the ascent was at a forty-five degree grade.

Yet, at the moment, Chilkoot Pass was not their problem. Unnoticed while they rushed to land their goods, the sky had become overcast and a chill drizzle had begun to fall. Misery loves company, and there was a certain amount of comfort in the fact that they were not alone on the low tidal beach. At least a thousand people were there ahead of them, sorting and squabbling over a mountain of goods dumped at the high-water mark with no ceremony and little order. Men and women were trying to lay claim to their goods and make some sense of the chaos. A tent city blossomed on site, and some of the new arrivals had fallen, exhausted, on their bales or were lying asleep on the sand beside the ten-foot mountain of stores, oblivious to the steady rain saturating their clothing.

"Doesn't look like there's any place left to store this stuff under cover, but I think I'll take a quick look, anyway," Brandon said.

"I'll stand guard here." Conrad sat on a box and used a flat rock in a futile attempt to scrape the caked mud from his legs. "It'll be dark in an hour," he added, glancing at the lowering sky.

"Well, you gents seem to have things well in hand," Saunderson said, his eyes crinkling in what Brandon took to be silent mirth.

"I sure appreciate your helping us lug all this ashore," Conrad said, holding out several folded bills.

"Hell, I didn't do it for money, son," Saunderson said, waving the greenbacks aside. "You Cheechakos look like you might have the makings. This country needs more men like you."

"Well, thanks," Conrad said, obviously flattered. "But I don't expect you to work for nothing."

"Son, I ain't braggin', but I could buy and sell both of you and all this food and gear with the nuggets I've got in my pocket. I do as I please. And right now it pleases me to give you a hand."

"Well, thanks a lot, Mister Saunderson."

"The name is Bob, but I ain't even answered to that in years. Some call me Wolverine Bob on account of a little dust-up with one o' them critters a few winters back. My good friends just call me Wolve or Sandy."

Conrad accepted this invitation of friendship with a nod.

Brandon silently resolved to get the story behind this moniker later.

"Anyhow, it was good to make your acquaintance," Wolve Saunderson said, extending his hand. "Maybe we'll see each other later on the trail."

"I hope so. Thanks again."

"Apparently didn't know who he was dealing with," Brandon chuckled softly as the big man ambled off. "Saying he could buy *you*."

Conrad grinned. "I wouldn't want to argue the point with him. His assets are probably not all tied up in buildings and machinery." Conrad's expression turned serious. "Don't say anything about me. As far as anyone else needs to know, I'm just another stampeder from the States. Conrad could be either my first or last name."

Brandon nodded his understanding. "I'll see if I can get my tent spread over some of this perishable stuff while you look for better shelter."

Twenty minutes later Brandon was back, feeling better than he had since leaving Louisville. His fatigue was gone, his heavy muddy feet light, and he didn't even care that his woolen jacket was soaked through.

"What's the big grin for?" Conrad asked, slipping out from under the corner of the white canvas tent that covered part of his pile. "You found gold already?"

"Almost as good. I ran across two parties who took a look at those mountains and decided it was time to sell out at a discount and go home."

"Really?"

"Yeah. I bought all kinds of stuff for about thirty percent of what it's really worth. I've finally got an outfit."

"Well, let's get busy and get it down here before they change their minds," Conrad said. "It's near dark. Looks like we'll have to camp out here tonight."

"Does that mean we're partners?" Brandon asked.

"If you can stand it for a little longer, I guess I can."

CHAPTER
FIVE

We landed in wind-swept Skagway.
We joined the weltering mass,
Clamoring over their outfits,
waiting to climb the Pass.
We tightened our girths and our pack-straps;
we linked on the Human Chain,
Struggling up to the summit,
where every step was a pain.
Gone was the joy of our faces,
grim and haggard and pale;
The heedless mirth of the shipboard
was changed to the care of the trail . . .
Robert Service

"I've got my initials marked on nearly every one of these boxes and bags, but that won't mean anything if I'm not here to defend them," Conrad said the next morning.

They were sipping coffee boiled over a small fire. The fire had been an accomplishment — built of wet wood from a splintered packing box. The high tide lapped at the sand five yards from a ten-foot-high ridge of supplies piled along the beach. Dozens of cooking fires added a smudgy layer to the murky morning overcast.

"The next problem is to get all this over the mountain and down to the lakes as quick as we can,"

Brandon said. He spoke with a freshness he didn't feel. In fact, he'd slept poorly in his wet clothes, and felt a little feverish. His eyes and throat were irritated. He sipped the scalding black coffee without relish.

"We might be better off to buy some pack horses and take the longer, lower trail over White Pass," Conrad said.

He spoke of buying a string of horses as casually as Brandon might have said he was going to buy a half dozen pairs of socks.

"Everybody who brought livestock will have to go that way," Brandon said. As soon as gray daylight began stealing over the makeshift camp before four o'clock, the piles of goods began to move, trickling away on hand carts, back packs, horse-drawn sledges, small wagons pulled by dogs. But mostly supplies were hauled on human backs — both white and Indian.

"Since you're in better shape than I am, why don't you go over to Skagway and check out that other trail. If it looks more promising, we'll ferry the goods over there, get some horses, and give it a try."

Brandon groaned inwardly. His first major test. He was tired and feverish and aching. He felt like getting into a hot bath, and a dry bed — anything but taking a long hike. But not by a flicker of an eyelash would he have let on how he felt. Except for the pile of goods he'd bought for thirty cents on the dollar and hauled down the beach, he owed everything to Milton Conrad.

"Sure," Brandon replied quickly. "That trail's at least twenty miles to the summit. I'll follow it until I get a good idea of what it's like."

"Follow it far enough to see if it's more feasible than Chilkoot. We already know Chilkoot's a killer."

"Where are you going to be?"

"Right here. I'll try to find us some kind of transportation. Maybe Indian packers. I don't feel like doing a lot of back-tripping myself."

"Let's say I meet you here tomorrow night. I think I can be there and back by then." Brandon pitched the bitter dregs of coffee from the enameled cup. He strapped on the Bisley Colt under his jacket, dug into a couple of the boxes for a stick of dried beef and a handful of prunes, slung a canteen over his shoulder, thrust a handful of sulphur matches into his side pocket, and started up the beach. "If I'm not back in forty-eight hours, better come looking for me," he added over his shoulder.

Brandon carried a map, torn from a guidebook he'd picked up in Chicago — a map that traced the trails from the coast to the interior. But it gave little information about the relative merits of the various routes. By making a few inquiries, he found that a steam ferry plied between Dyea and Skagway. He splashed knee-deep through icy water for a hundred yards before he caught a ride on a scow transporting a last load of goods to the ferry. Then, finding a place in the sun out of the wind, he clasped his arms and shivered, hoping the sun would dry his pants and warm him up.

Skagway was a settlement fast outgrowing its housing and blooming with more tents than buildings. The main part of the settlement was composed of one- and

62

two-story frame structures. This place seemed even more crowded with newcomers and their goods than Dyea. Built mostly of warping green lumber, the buildings lined streets laid out in a grid pattern. Another of those shoal-draft towns, Brandon noted, but not as bad as Dyea. Skagway did have one pier and a harbor just deep enough for the flat-bottomed steam ferry to berth alongside it. A gang of men was busy constructing an extension to the dock while a steam dredge was digging up piles of muck to deepen the harbor.

He lost no time in finding the beginning of the trail on the edge of town. In spite of his heavy, muddy boots, he took off at a jogging pace to get himself warmed up. Alternately running and walking, he passed a steady line of pack animals, cattle, and hiking stampeders heading for the mountain. For the first several miles the trail had only a gradual ascent through a forest. A cold rain began to fall again, and the trail, churned up by thousands of boots and hoofs, was a black, sticky mire. Most of the time he had to run alongside the trail in the edge of the woods to keep his footing. He came to places where the trail was blocked by cattle and pack horses sunk to their bellies in the goo, while their owners pushed and prodded and cursed and pulled, trying to extricate them. Others behind them shouted and cursed and tried to squeeze their own animals past. The trail roughly paralleled the Skagway River and skirted low, swampy areas, while in other spots crossed a ford on the rocks. As the ascent grew steeper, and rockier, the stench of dead flesh assaulted his nostrils in the humid air. He caught his breath as he came upon literally hundreds of dead horses, mules, and cattle along several miles of trail where they had slipped and fallen on the sharp rocks and been left to die or been shot. In two places, he had to detour fifty yards out of his way to avoid having to walk on the rotting carcasses. Many of the dead bodies were nothing but shredded hide and bones where they had been tromped into the mud by the relentless stream of humans and animals that followed.

Even though he was in fair athletic condition, his legs felt sapped of strength; he couldn't believe he was worn out already. He sat down to rest on a tree stump, his chest heaving and his stomach rebelling at the stench. As soon as he stopped moving, mosquitoes began whining around his ears. He was caked with mud to the knees and dared not take off his lace-up boots here to examine his feet. He felt blisters had formed inside his wet socks and decided to buy or trade for a pair of high rubber boots to keep his feet dry in the future. He brushed away a black fly biting the back of his hand.

While Brandon rested, two men came down the trail toward Skagway. One led a pack horse that carried an empty pack saddle.

"Hey, gents, what's the trail like up above?"

They paused. The man with a beard shoved his hat back on his head. "You don't wanna know."

"More of the same, only worse," the second man chimed in. "They don't call this the Dead Horse Trail for nothing. Steeper, rockier, muddier. You can make it afoot if you're careful. For long stretches you could walk on nothing but carcasses if you was of a mind. You ain't carrying a load. That helps."

The bearded one suppressed a grin. "Hope you're packin' your own grub."

"All the game scared off?"

"Any edible critters have pretty much scattered," he agreed. "But there's a restaurant on top of the pass. Fella that runs it is making do with what Providence provides."

"How so?" Brandon slapped a mosquito that had lighted on his cheek.

"He serves the freshest steaks for forty miles around. But we're mighty suspicious that he gets his meat supply free from the carcasses of cattle and horses just down the trail from his establishment."

"Enterprising."

"You might say so. Anyhow, since 'most everybody with pack animals and livestock has to take this route, I'd advise going the other way up Chilkoot Pass."

"Obliged."

The two men continued down the trail.

Brandon didn't have a watch, but he estimated by the dull light filtering through the overcast that it was at least three in the afternoon. He figured he had covered half the distance to the summit and decided there was no use going farther.

During the twenty minutes or so he had rested, his muscles had chilled and stiffened. He got up, stretched, and sipped some water from his canteen to fool his grumbling stomach. Then he started back down the trail at a ground-eating lope. He'd had a substantial breakfast several hours before and needed to condition himself to go longer without food.

As long as he was moving, the black flies and mosquitoes didn't swarm around him. He could imagine that the irritating bites of these pests were one of the things which had driven the slow-moving oxen and horses to bolt off the muddy trail or miss their footing and fall down the rocky gorges.

Seeing how the trail curved, he thought to take a short cut and save himself some distance. Gauging with his eye about where he would come out on the trail lower down, he set off through the woods. He was quickly out of sight and sound of the trail and, after a half-hour, began to get the uneasy feeling he had somehow missed the trail he had hoped to intersect. The leaden overcast gave him no hint of direction by the sun. Hot and thirsty after plunging through some thick vines and undergrowth, he paused to catch his breath and swat away the clouds of mosquitoes that were swarming about his head. He found himself standing beside some bushes that were loaded with ripe blueberries. "Like Adam in paradise," he muttered, helping himself to a small handful of the sweet, tart fruit. He washed them down with water from his canteen. A few minutes later, refreshed, he started again, and managed to blunder his way onto the trail about twenty minutes later.

Jogging and walking, he reached Skagway again by nine in the evening. The overcast had begun to clear, and the sun was still visible above the western horizon. The long summer twilight would last until nearly midnight. By some diligent inquiries, he finally found a cot to rent in a partially built wooden hotel that was using canvas for walls. He couldn't sleep with the sun still up, so he went for supper — beef stew at $2.00 a bowl. At a nearby store, he outfitted himself with a pair of knee-high rubber boots. Guessing at Conrad's size, he also bought a pair for his partner.

Later that night, before the late-setting sun was fairly down, he was sound asleep, his wet clothes and boots piled under the cot. It was first time he'd been dry all day.

The ferry back to Dyea didn't pull out until ten o'clock next morning, and Brandon was anxious to be on it. He'd seen quite enough of the White Pass Trail and of Skagway. The town was a dreary collection of frame buildings about equally divided between newly constructed residences and stores, saloons, gambling houses, and hotels, the last bursting at the seams with stampeders. White tents were everywhere on the edges of town. Even from the vantage point of the waterfront, Skagway had a raw appearance — muddy streets still decorated with fresh tree stumps, unpainted wooden buildings thrown up as fast as carpenters could swing a hammer, pine boards still oozing sap. The whole place smelled of fresh resin and aromatic wood smoke that overrode the dead fish and manure smells beneath. Saloons were open and booming twenty-four hours a day. Even at mid-morning, they were doing a good business.

He wondered what had happened to Annie and George O'Connell. Was the old man an alcoholic? Had they gone on to meet their party in Chicago? Or had they given up their gold quest as a bad idea and returned home to Cincinnati?

He shook his head as he stood waiting for the ferry to begin boarding. If a man had a weakness for strong drink, he would likely never get beyond these man-trap saloons. But from stories he'd heard of earlier gold rushes in the West, conditions were ever the same. In this mix of humanity were con men, prostitutes, robbers, and murderers. Many snares awaited the feet of the weak and the unwary. He had no inkling that his thoughts were to prove prophetic.

CHAPTER
SIX

Oh, we were brutes and devils,
goaded by lust and fear!
Our eyes were strained to the summit;
the weaklings dropped to the rear,
Falling in heaps by the trail-side,
heartbroken, limp and wan;
But the gaps closed up in an instant,
and heedless the chain went on.
Robert Service

"What the hell happened, Wolve?" Brandon searched the face of the bearded Saunderson as the two men stepped outside the North Star Hotel in Dyea. "Who beat up my partner?" He was nearly trembling with anger, and had to force his voice to remain steady.

"Wal, you're not going to like my answer," the big man drawled, removing the stubby briar from his mouth and turning to spit into the muddy street. "I didn't see this myself, o' course, but here's the way I got the story from an Injun I trust. It's a familiar tale."

Brandon shifted his weight, but forced himself to be patient.

"It was one o' Soapy Smith's men named Shiv Mulette who lured Conrad into that shed behind Doyle's place. Two of his friends . . . Big Ed Burns and Yank Hank Fewclothes . . . jumped him there, the Injun said. Beat him pretty bad and took his poke. When we carried him into the hotel here, I see they even knocked out his gold tooth. His face was all swole up, and I think they might've kicked in a couple of ribs."

"How could he have been so gullible?" Brandon groaned.

"Oh, Soapy's men are slick. They've conned more experienced men than your partner. They mostly prey on Cheechakos like yourselves. No offense . . ."

"What could this Shiv Mulette have said that lured him away from guarding our goods?"

Saunderson shrugged. "Could have been anything. Offered him a free drink, sold him a map to get a look at his billfold, saw what kind of clothes or weapons he had, to see if he had money, offered to lead him to some cheap Injun packers . . . could have been most anything."

"Who the hell is this Soapy Smith, anyway?"

"Jefferson Randolph Smith is his real moniker. Crook out of Colorado, I hear. He and a half dozen men came here one jump ahead of the law. Soapy's got himself set up at a place called Clancy's Saloon over in Skagway. I understand he's building a place of his own with the cash he's fleeced or robbed. There ain't no end to his schemes. If you stay around here, you'll hear a lot about Soapy Smith . . . and it's not all bad. There're lots of folks who swear by his generosity . . . widows and people down on their luck, prospectors he's staked . . ."

"All with somebody else's money."

70

"Just tellin' ya the way it is. Probably why he hasn't been snatched up to a tree limb by a vigilance committee by now. Some think he's a modern Robin Hood."

"Shit!"

"The suckers he lures into his saloon and cheats, or those he has followed and mugged, can't prove he's behind it, or that his gambling tables are crooked. If a victim hollers too loud, or threatens violence, he simply disappears."

"How long has he been getting away with all this?"

"Ever since he came here . . . a few weeks back. Just before I went Outside to the States."

"It's time somebody put a stop to Mister Soapy Jefferson Randolph Smith," Brandon said grimly, hitching up his gun belt. "Think I'll take the ferry back to Skagway and pay him a visit."

"I'd leave him alone, if I was you. Your partner's not too bad hurt. Get him on his feet in a week or so and get over the mountain while the weather is still good. You've got a ways to go to Dawson, and a lot of grub to pack. You came here for gold. Get on with it. Don't get yourself sidetracked and maybe killed. This land will be enough of an enemy, come winter."

Brandon considered the advice, his outrage still burning inside. He tried to shut out the hate and focus on the immediate problems. "They got all the money he had. I have only about fifty left."

"If you want my advice, I'd sell off some o' that mountain o' goods you got. Do it after you get past the Mounties on the summit of Chilkoot. Appears you got more'n you need. It'd give you some cash to operate on."

"Thanks. I hadn't thought of that. I'm so damned mad, I'm not thinking straight." Brandon clenched his fists at his sides.

"This ain't no place to be doin' that, even for a little while. There'll be times when your life will depend on you having a cool head. Take it from me, this land don't give no compromises."

"I still can't stand the idea of somebody getting away with assault and robbery."

"Chalk it up to experience. Soapy and his boys will get their come-uppance soon enough." He knocked his pipe against his boot heel.

"I guess you're right. This is a lawless country. And I'm not equipped right now to put things right. But I won't forget."

"Nobody's askin' ya to," Wolve Saunderson said evenly. He paused and looked down the street. "I'd be glad to give you a hand packin' your stuff. But your partner won't be able to travel for a week or more, and I have to meet my partner in Dawson."

"We already owe you a lot for your help."

"You'll find that folks who've been in this country for a while don't offer help for pay . . . except maybe an Injun packer, or some such. This country's so big and harsh that we poor humans just naturally tend to reach out a helping hand to one another. Not like the crowds in the cities Outside where everybody's in competition for themselves. That may all change with the thousands o' Cheechakos pouring in now." He spat into the

72

muddy street. "And, o' course, you have a few skunks like Soapy Smith and his boys. But, so far, they're so few they stick out like a wart on your nose."

Brandon was silent for several seconds, pondering the situation. "If the last part of that trail up Chilkoot is as steep and tough, as they say, I think I'll sell off some of our goods here, instead of packing them all over the mountain and then selling them. We could use the cash to pay for some Indian packers."

"Good idea," Saunderson said. "Just one little catch. Those Mounties at the customs post aren't going to let you through unless you got two thousand pounds of supplies per man."

"What about you?"

He waved a hand. "Hell, they know me on sight. I been here longer than any of them. I'm already established on the Yukon. The Mounties are just trying to keep from having to rescue all these newcomers who don't know what they're doing."

"I think I know a way to get around the Mountie check," Brandon said reflectively.

Over the next few hours, Brandon quickly advertised, up and down Dyea beach, that he was selling at a good price. He'd hoped to get approximately what the goods had cost in the States, but, for the next two days, the competition of returning parties forced the price down, so that he eventually settled for less than half what he guessed the load was worth. But every time he took a loss, he consoled himself with the thought that there was another fifty or hundred pounds of bacon or beans or flour or a six-foot saw that he would not have to pack on his back, or pay someone else to pack. The instinct to travel light still strove to master him.

"Hold 'er there, Terry," Wolve Saunderson said, coming along the beach just as Brandon was showing off his snow-shoes and a ten-foot sled. "You don't want to be cuttin' it too thin."

"You're right." Brandon waved off his prospective customer. He looked around at the remaining heap that was partially covered by the canvas tent. "Still looks like a lot." He was not good at estimating weights. Thus he was ignorant of the inordinate amount of food and gear that Milton Conrad had bought and hauled with him, plus what he himself had purchased when they first landed.

"Believe me, you'll need most o' that."

"Conrad!" Brandon saw his partner approaching from several yards off, walking in a bent posture and holding his side like some old man. He went to help him to a sitting position on a box.

"He's still pretty shaky on his pins," Saunderson said. "But I got him outta bed and paid off the hotel. Nellie Cashman wouldn't take nothing for stitching his head and tending to him. That woman's an angel in a calico dress."

"Who's she? I need at least to thank her," Brandon said.

"She come up here from the States where she used to run a boardin' house. Plans to do the same in Dawson like she done in Tombstone. But the point is she's like a mother to all miners and men away from home. Kindness itself. She can cook and nurse like nobody's business. Some folks got a green thumb for growing things. Nellie's got a healing touch and a big heart."

"I hope to meet her," Brandon said. Then he turned to Conrad. "How're you feeling? You don't look like you're up to traveling."

"Give me a day or so, and I think I can manage," he said. He was still holding his ribs and seemed a little breathless.

"Nellie bound him up pretty tight. Said to leave it on for a week. He'll have some trouble taking a deep breath for a few days. Won't be able to carry much besides himself, but I think he'll mend all right."

"I can't thank you enough," Conrad said, reaching out to take Saunderson's hand. The big man's ruddy complexion deepened a shade or two. "You can thank me by getting on the outside of some grub and bucking up for the trail. Old man winter don't wait for no man." He looked at both of them. "Sorry I can't stay to help, but I gotta pull outta here first thing tomorrow. I hope to see you both downriver before freeze-up." With that, he shouldered his pack and trudged away toward town.

CHAPTER
SEVEN

**Floundering deep in the sump-holes,
stumbling out again;
Crying with cold and weakness,
crazy with fear and pain.
Then from the depths of our travail,
ere our spirits were broke,
Grim, tenacious and savage,
the lust of the trail awoke.**
Robert Service

It was three long weeks before Milton Conrad was ready for the trail. With little help from his injured partner, Brandon pulled the white tent off their remaining pile of goods and set up the canvas shelter. Then he made the interior as comfortable as possible. Beyond that, there was little he could do except fret at the delay. Each day he watched more and more stampeders start up the trail toward the mountain, hauling their supplies on horses, makeshift carts, sleds with wheels attached, but mostly human backs. He looked on every one of them — even women and the city-bred men who were ill-equipped for the task — as potential rivals. They would all be on their claims, digging and panning out gold nuggets long before he and Conrad arrived. All the good places would be staked. Indeed, all the gold-bearing claims might already be taken. He had to console himself with the thought that this was a vast country, and no man was an expert at finding gold. From all he'd heard and seen, luck was as much a factor as skill or knowledge of geology. Even if all the rivers and creeks were staked, top to bottom, who was to say that the precious metal was not to be found in the hills and upland valleys? The gold had been ground into dust and small nuggets as it washed down from higher ground into the waterways. There could be a lot of it left in the hills. It would just require more digging and effort to get at it. And one would have to be lucky to pick the right spot; a prospector couldn't dig up the whole country.

Thus he spent hours and days sitting on a packing case outside their tent and mulling over the possibilities. But the itch to get going wouldn't allow him really to sit still. It wasn't just the stampeders who were trickling past him into town and out onto the Chilkoot Trail. With each passing day, implacable winter was sliding down from the tip of the planet as the earth tilted away from the sun. Wolve Saunderson had put it best: "Old man winter don't wait for no man." Easy-going though Saunderson was in most things, he spoke soberly of the coming winter. Traveling by boat down to Dawson should be relatively easy. But getting over the pass, then hiking down the few miles to the first connected lake with their gear, and building a boat would all take time. And while Conrad recuperated in the tent with agonizing slowness, time was sliding away from them like the thin cirrus clouds overhead.

Each day brought some improvement in his wealthy partner's condition. The swelling in his face gradually subsided, and in less than a week they were able to snip and extract the stitches from his scalp. Two red scars still showed in the white skin where Nellie Cashman had shaved the black hair to get at his wounds.

"Hell, I wear my hat most of the time, anyway," Conrad had said when Brandon joshed him about his lopsided appearance. "As for this missing tooth . . . well, I'll just replace it with gold from the first nugget we find." He showed a gapped grin still slightly crooked from the discolored swelling in his right cheek.

After the first five days, they walked up and down the beach, and Conrad was definitely regaining his strength. By the end of the week, his appetite and ability to chew showed signs of returning, and Brandon progressed from giving him broth and tiny bits of bread to something more substantial.

When they carefully unwound the bandages from his torso at the end of a week, Brandon saw how thin — almost gaunt — Conrad was. But, for the first time, he took a few tentative deep breaths. The soreness was still there, but the ribs were on the mend.

That afternoon, while Brandon was in town, Conrad rummaged through a box of personal items he'd packed, digging out several sheets of writing paper, a bottle of ink, and his fountain pen. Except for a hurried letter posted from Seattle, he'd not written his wife Judith as he promised he would. The rays of the afternoon sun were slanting into the tent when he sat down on a packing case, using another box for a desk, and began to to collect his thoughts. This letter must have the right tone to allay all worries.

Dearest Judy & Steven,

I'm writing you from Dyea, on the coast of Alaska. I've discovered that a man alone stands little chance of success in this country, so I've partnered up with a man from Kentucky. I firmly believe he'll be a great asset in my search for gold. His name is Terry Brandon and we are of a similar age, and he is very athletic. I helped him out with his steamship fare, and it has proven so far to be an excellent investment. I wouldn't be surprised if we turned out to be good friends.

He paused, pen poised, trying to form his thoughts. He had never been one to verbalize his inner feelings. The men in his family were reticent when it came to displaying emotion.

As you know, I started on this trip trying to escape, or delay, a future that was rushing upon me with a suffocating suddenness. I feel that I will have to follow through with my quest for gold. That quest may last a few more weeks or even several months. It is difficult to predict because I've already seen that this country is big and beautiful and brutal. Our goal is to get our goods across the mountain and down the Yukon River somewhere near the town of Dawson before winter sets in, which it does early here.

He hesitated, wondering if he should mention his beating. Yes — he should be honest with her, regardless of the anguish it might cause. When she saw that he could surmount any obstacle on his own, without the help of powerful relatives, she would think even more of him.

I've had a small personal setback. I was attacked and beaten by three thugs who stole my ready cash. I received some cuts on my head and bruised ribs but am recovering nicely. Don't worry about me. We have more than enough food and equipment and will sell some of it for whatever ready cash we might need.

As you can see from this, there are both bad and good people in this horde of gold-seekers, and we have encountered both. One old sourdough named Saunderson has been both friend and benefactor. In fact, he got the best care for me after my injuries and paid the cost himself. If you think the world of business is rough and tumble, you haven't see anything. You can't imagine the chaotic situation of thousands of stampeders overwhelming what little civilization exists on the Alaskan coast. The rules of decency and order are pretty much ignored, except by those who bring their morals in tact with them. I hear the

Canadians have a better grip on things just across the mountain.

With the help of some horses and Indian packers, Terry and I will begin carrying our supplies toward the mountain pass in a few days. I am posting this letter from here before we start to take advantage of U.S. mail service. Write to me in care of General Delivery, Skagway, Alaska Territory. Because we will be going into the interior, the mail may be very sporadic, so please do not worry about me if you don't hear anything further for several weeks.

He paused, scanning what he'd written. It almost sounded like a business letter.

I've seen lots of sights and had some adventure already, but if I had known how empty life would be without you, I would have brought you both along. (Yes, I've even seen families with children here.) I don't know if they are seeking gold, or are looking for a new life here in the North. I do know that here I feel free from all the constraints and expectations of my social and business life. I don't miss that one bit, but I <u>really</u> miss you and Steven. Is he crawling yet? It seems like forever since I've seen both of you. I have never been good at expressing my feelings, but know that you and the baby are in my thoughts every waking hour. Somehow I feel this is going to be the greatest adventure of my life, and I know I'll return to you a better husband and father than when I left.

If, God forbid, anything should happen to me, go on with the knowledge that I was trying to find a better life for us.

Love,
Milton

Conrad debated whether or not to scratch out that last sentence. But, given the danger and uncertainty, he decided to leave it in order to prepare her for any eventuality. He addressed it, sealed the envelope, and gave it to Brandon that evening to post for him the next day.

When he wasn't tending his partner, Brandon was making all the preparations he could for the trail. He went through their supplies, discarding perishable food that had gone bad, trimming mold off sides of bacon, repacking large boxes down into more manageable sizes, cleaning and oiling their leather boots.

One afternoon, when he returned from having the worst of their dirty clothes washed in a laundry in town, he found Conrad in the tent, doing some stretching and bending exercises that had been part of his regimen for several days.

"I think I'll be ready to go by tomorrow," he announced, straightening up. "Let's make a go at getting this stuff hauled up at least as far as Sheep Camp so we can be ready for the climb over the pass."

It was the news Brandon had been waiting to hear; he'd been at the point of suggesting he start packing the goods by himself. The first week of September had already passed, and the days were rapidly growing shorter. "I believe we've got enough money for at least two horses. I'll see what I can find, then I'll look for Indian packers, too," he added, throwing back the tent flap and starting for town.

He was back before supper, leading two horses with wooden pack saddles. "Best I could do, with the money I had," he apologized as Conrad ran his hands over the animals' tendons and inspected the scars on their backs from some past galling. The horses had obviously been worked before and were not fractious, so there should be no problem in handling them.

Anxious to be off, Brandon went out into the lingering twilight to see if he could hire some native packers. He had long since found out where they congregated in Dyea. But finding them and hiring them were two entirely different matters. The two most common native tribes in this area of southern coastal Alaska were the Tlingits and the Aleuts. From what he'd seen, the former were here in much greater numbers. Most of the Tlingit men were short and stocky, had Mongolian features, and sported drooping mustaches. Both the men and women seemed eager and able to pack for the white stampeders.

Brandon had no interpreter, but most of these Indians, from frequent contact with white men, had learned a smattering of English — at least, enough to communicate on a rudimentary basis. And, as Brandon quickly found out, they had learned other things as well, including how to bargain like the toughest union bosses.

"I need packers," Brandon began. "Strong men. Maybe six men to haul goods to Sheep Camp."

Two thick-chested men, standing by the village scales, looked at each other and conversed briefly in their native tongue.

"Ten cents a pound," Brandon offered when they looked back at him. He'd been told early on that this was the going rate.

One of the men, who looked decidedly Oriental, laughed. "No . . . no. We strong. Fifty cents."

Brandon's stomach sank, but he never flinched. "Fifteen cents," he said.

The two men looked at each other and shook their heads. "Forty-five cents," one of them said.

"Twenty," Brandon countered.

The two natives seemed to think this was hugely funny. They laughed and spoke rapidly to each other. Brandon felt he was at a great disadvantage and wished Wolve Saunderson were here. Even if the big man couldn't do anything directly, at least he could lend some moral support. He was sure the old sourdough would have more influence on these packers than a Cheechako would have.

"You pay forty cents a pound," the taller of the pair said.

"Twenty-five," Brandon offered.

"Forty."

"Too much."

One of the Indians shrugged, and the pair turned away.

"OK. OK. Forty it is," Brandon agreed in desperation, trying to calculate in his head how much that amounted to. It was probably more than their whole outfit had cost, but there was no alternative other than struggling up and down the trail innumerable times, wasting additional days, and wearing themselves out. Because of the exorbitant price that supply and demand had forced on the market, Brandon was able to hire only the two men he'd been talking with.

True to their word, they were at the beach at five the next morning, loaded their home-made pack frames, and trudged off with Brandon to the town scales. Conrad stayed behind to pack the horses — a task, he later admitted, that took him a lot longer than it should have because it was strictly trial and error.

Brandon piled their sled high and lashed the load, then rigged a padded harness for himself across his chest and shoulders. It was a load he estimated he could drag over the mud and wet grass without wearing himself out in the first mile. Finally the little party of four men, two horses, and a sled set out on the trail to Sheep Camp, leaving at least half of their supplies piled on the beach.

The muggy air and the exertion caused Brandon to break into a sweat after a few hundred yards. The sled did not slide easily over dry ground and rocks. His damp woolen clothing began to itch, and the harness straps chafed. Over the first two miles on nearly level terrain, he was able to find enough slick mud to pull the loaded sled. Then the trail began to climb slightly and become drier and rockier. He was compelled to stop more frequently to rest and readjust the make-shift shoulder harness. The others in his party stopped to wait for him, but he waved them on.

"I'll catch up later. Get to Sheep Camp and come back for another load."

Brandon watched the phlegmatic Indians turn and plod on ahead, leading the pack horses. He wished he could have afforded to buy another horse to pull this sled. Conrad seemed to be favoring his ribs as he leaned forward under his load and disappeared around a turn in the trail. Brandon pulled the sled to one side, and other hikers flowed past like water in an interrupted stream. A light mist had turned into a steady, cold drizzle, and still he sat on the sled, catching his breath and wondering if he would be able to haul this load another several miles to the village of Sheep Camp, near the base of the Chilkoot Pass. He'd gone only about two miles, and already he was looking over his load with an eye to getting rid of some things on the sled he'd earlier considered indispensable.

He climbed to his feet and slipped the harness over his aching shoulders to start again. Two stampeders came back-tripping down the trail, one of them pulling an empty hand-made cart with two solid wooden wheels. The wheels, cross sections of a tree, were about two feet in diameter and three inches thick, reinforced against splitting with diagonal strips of wood.

"Hey, you done with that cart?" he asked on a sudden whim.

The man paused. "Not quite yet."

"How much will you take for it right now?" Brandon asked quickly.

"I need it for one more load," the man said.

"Hell, sell it, Dick," his companion chipped in. "We can pack the rest of that stuff on our backs. We won't have no use for that cart getting over the pass, anyhow."

"Twenty dollars," the first man said.

Brandon reached into his side pocket and took out a double eagle, handing it over before the man could change his mind or raise the price.

"Nice doin' business with ya," the man nodded, and the pair went on down the trail.

Brandon quickly unloaded the sled and packed everything on the cart. Piled high, it nearly all fit. Then he manhandled the sled across the top of the load and lashed it in place. The whole thing was awkward and top heavy, but at least he now had wheels under it all. Strange as it looked, he found it much easier to pull. The Indian packers, the horses, and Conrad were already out of sight ahead, but that didn't concern him. What did concern him was the cold rain that was now falling harder. As he leaned into the harness, water dripped off his hat brim, and he felt the chill wetness soaking through the shoulders of his coat.

Three hours later, he saw the village of Sheep Camp ahead with its frame buildings, shacks, and tents. The tiny settlement was bulging with stampeders who had paused to collect themselves for the final assault on

Chilkoot Pass. The whole scene reminded Brandon of a slow, flotsam-choked stream beginning to pool up behind an earthen dam.

He caught up with the others where they had unloaded the pack horses, and the Indians began to help Conrad set up their white canvas tent to cover the supplies.

"Feel like making another trip?" He looked at Conrad whose pinched face and stooped posture told him the answer.

"Sure!" Conrad seemed to force a grin that showed the gap in his teeth.

"Maybe you should stay here and watch this stuff. I'll go back with the packers and horses. Don't overtax yourself. We can manage without you for now."

"Why don't we all wait until morning?" Conrad suggested, tugging on a guy rope to tighten the sagging canvas. "It'll be dark before you get back."

Brandon shook his head. "Don't want to lose the packers now that we've got 'em. One more load should do it, since we sold all that stuff."

"Well . . . OK." Conrad, favoring his side, went inside out of the rain and sat down on a box.

Tired as he was, Brandon signaled the Indians, picked up the handles of the two-wheeled cart, and started back down the trail at a jog. Pride was part of the reason for his show of freshness, but he also wanted to get this over with before he sat down and stiffened up. He grudgingly admitted to himself that these natives were in much better shape for this sort of work. Athletic he might be, but his muscles were not conditioned for hours on end of pushing, pulling, and carrying.

They reached the beach at Dyea late in the afternoon, and loaded up the rest of their gear. Each Indian's pack, when he set it on the scales, registered between a hundred and thirty and a hundred and forty pounds. Brandon had learned quickly about the proper way to secure a load on a horse's pack saddle. When the two-wheeled cart was filled to the maximum he could pull, there were still a few odds and ends left behind, but he had estimated fairly accurately.

The trail back toward the mountain was muddier and just as crowded with a steady stream of hikers. On the narrower, rockier parts, Brandon and the two Tlingits were held up by slower stampeders ahead. The rain kept pounding, and an early darkness began to settle in where the trail wound through stands of tall spruce. All along the well-trodden path Brandon saw remnants of small trees that had been hacked off for firewood, shelter poles, hiking sticks, and whatever else the human horde needed.

As the trail steepened, he slipped and slid, tearing a hole in his rubber boots on a sharp rock. Then he wet his legs to the knees while crossing the shallow river ford. It had been full dark for an hour when they finally came in sight of the few low fires of Sheep Camp. After stowing the gear in the tent, Brandon paid off the Indian packers with double eagles. They examined the coins in the firelight and tested the gold with their teeth before they grunted their affirmation and disappeared into the night.

Since they had no grain or hay to feed the horses, Brandon led the animals among the tents, hawking them for sale. He received only one offer, and it was for less than he wanted, but he sold them anyway.

"Think it was wise to let those Indian packers go?" Conrad asked, two hours later as he sat staring into the flames of the small campfire in front of their tent.

"They wanted another forty cents a pound just to get us over the pass," Brandon replied, setting aside his tin plate, wiped clean of bacon and beans. "We can't afford it."

Conrad gave him a weak grin. "I never thought I'd be in a situation where I'd have to worry about money." His partially healed injuries and today's long hike under a heavy pack seemed to have taken all the fire out of him. Brandon glanced sideways, wondering if his partner's spirit was sagging along with his body. Brandon knew they should have waited at least another week to let Conrad's broken ribs heal, but the seasons were inexorably changing. They could not delay any longer if they were to reach Dawson before the freeze-up.

"Only about four miles to go to the summit tomorrow," Brandon said, smoothing the map on his knee and peering closely at it in the flickering firelight. "The last half mile is the toughest . . . a climb of a thousand feet."

Conrad fed the blaze with a splintered stick of scrap wood. "We'll get an early start," he said. His voice lacked energy. "I'm bushed. Think I'll hit the sack. Wake me at daylight."

"Who's going to wake *me?*" Brandon grinned ruefully, feeling his stiffening muscles and the leaden weight of fatigue.

Later, Brandon would credit the fever-ache of his broken sleep for saving them from disaster.

CHAPTER
EIGHT

> ...We voyaged Lake Bennett,
> Tagish then Windy Arm,
> Sinister savage and baleful,
> boding us hate and harm
> Many a scow was shattered
> there on that iron shore;
> Many a heart was broken straining
> at sweep and oar.
> Robert Service

Brandon rolled over, drowsily aware of his aching shoulder and back muscles. He tried to squirm into a more comfortable position, but distant screams ripped through his thin veil of sleep. It was a cry of terror that brought him fully awake and listening. More yells, along with crashing, clattering noises.

Brandon threw off his blanket, pulled on his rubber boots, and stepped outside the tent in his long underwear. Chill, damp air, but no rain. The blackness enveloped him while the racket assaulted his ears — rushing, smashing, punctuated by human cries. What was happening? Then he heard the unmistakable clatter of a clapboard house collapsing. An earthquake? He felt no movement of the ground under his boots. From somewhere below, a panicked shout reached his ears: "Flood!"

The cry chilled him. He felt the sudden cold rush of water swishing through the hole in his boot. He leaped back inside the tent. "Conrad! Wake up!" He shook his partner. "Flash flood! We have to get out!"

Conrad stumbled to his feet. "Need my clothes . . . ," he mumbled incoherently.

Brandon grabbed his own rolled up pants that'd been serving as a pillow. He scooped up his gun belt while Conrad pulled on his shirt.

"Let's go!" He heard Conrad gasp and grabbed his arm. They plunged into the cold water that swirled halfway to their knees, flooding the tent.

"High ground! Quick!" Brandon turned to run, tripped over the tent's guy rope, pulling the stake out of the ground. The tent began to collapse.

Conrad was apparently fully awake and lunging ahead of Brandon, both men struggling against thigh-deep water, swirling with débris.

They staggered up the slope and into shallower water. In less than a minute, they were safe on higher ground, gasping, looking back, trying to penetrate the darkness. Brandon sensed the grinding flow of boards, trees, boxes, and bales of every sort. Here and there the white blob of a tent showed vaguely.

"Where'd all that water come from?" Conrad gasped, leaning forward on his knees. "It's not even raining."

"Dunno. Flash flood from up the valley somewhere."

No moon or stars showed through the solid overcast, and Brandon could only guess at the destruction of Sheep Camp below them. He was trembling from exertion and the wet cold. He knew that all their goods that had cost so much in money and effort were probably washed away. "Shit!" he exploded. "Shit!"

They stood for a few minutes, sensing the grinding sweep of the mass of water and débris, moving down the valley at their feet.

"Let's find some shelter," Conrad said, turning uphill.

They stumbled blindly away, holding onto each other. Indistinct forms of other refugees were moving near them. At last, about ten of them came upon an empty log hut. A man with dry matches managed to light a coal-oil lamp he found inside. Drenched and in all stages of undress, men and women alike seemed dazed with shock as they stared numbly at each other in the soft yellow light of the lamp. Two men with matches vainly attempted to start a fire in the stone fireplace. They were able to ignite a few curls of wood they shaved from a log on the outdoor wood pile, but the larger pieces were too wet, and the hissing fire refused to blaze.

With the smoky lamp on the single small table, the bedraggled people huddled here and there on the floor, under a coat or shawl, husbands and wives hugging one another for warmth. Brandon and Conrad shared a soggy blanket someone offered them. It was probably not over two hours until dawn, but, to Brandon, the demons of darkness seemed determined to linger forever, hiding the destruction that an impersonal nature had inflicted on the valley.

The early sun struggled to penetrate the leaden overcast as Brandon stood outside the hut, damp blanket wrapped around his shoulders. The water had receded into the banks of the small river, but, judging from the trash caught in the tree limbs, the high water must have covered the entire village. It was now the *former* village of Sheep Camp. All that remained were scattered piles of rock where chimneys had stood, while both sides of the valley as far as he could see downstream were littered with the thousands of boards, boxes, and barrels, even the carcasses of horses, tents and clothing twisted around bushes.

As he looked, Conrad joined him, hugging himself against the damp chill of early morning. "All gone," he said in a hollow monotone.

Brandon nodded, hardly trusting himself to speak. Wolve Saunderson had not been overly dramatic when he had remarked that this country was unforgiving. As the light grew stronger, he saw that the floodwaters had not gotten everything. Apparently a number of the campers had received warning in time to carry some of their goods out of harm's way to higher ground. Men and women were stirring in the distance. He saw figures moving, heard the *thunk* of an axe, and saw smoke beginning to rise from several fires.

"Let's go see what we can find," he said to Conrad, trying to keep the discouragement out of his voice. All the effort and expense of buying and hauling more than a ton of supplies to the base of this mountain only to have it swept away in a twinkling was more than he could grasp. Was this some kind of omen? Maybe he should have aborted this trip long ago.

At least, he had his rubber boots on to protect his feet. He had slipped into his pants and buckled on his gun belt. Conrad was stuffing in his shirt tail. Brandon swung the damp blanket from his shoulders and tossed it back inside the hut before the two of them started back downhill.

They searched the area where Brandon knew their tent had stood. By some lucky chance, their sled with some of their clothing entangled in it had caught on a tree branch, and they managed to salvage a few items. A small, heavy box of ammunition was half-buried in the mud, and, wonder of wonders, Conrad's Marlin rifle was wedged between two rocks. The stock had sustained a deep gouge, but otherwise the weapon appeared undamaged except for water and mud.

A white-faced man in a long coat and boots approached. "The flood only got part of my stuff," the man said. "But I'm sellin' out and goin' back. This ain't no place for me. This is harder than workin' for a living." He paused to help Brandon pull the long sled off the jagged tree limb where it had snagged.

Brandon surveyed the wreckage of their few soggy belongings. "I guess we were just mighty lucky to get out with our lives," he consoled himself. "There wasn't any warning. It hadn't rained that much. Wonder what caused it?"

"Fella back yonder said an earth slide blocked the river upcañon a ways," said the man who was selling out. "Water built up behind it. When she let go, it all come down on us at once."

"Wish I could find my axe," Brandon said, noting that Conrad was shivering uncontrollably. "Need to split some kindling and get a fire going to dry out and warm up."

"I got an axe you can borrow," the man said. "Matter of fact, you can buy what's left of my outfit . . . cheap. All I want is enough for steamship passage home for me and the missus."

Brandon was suddenly thankful he'd had the foresight to grab his pants with his money in the pockets as he fled the rising water. "Sounds good to me. Where's your camp?"

They followed the man along the muddy riverbank, while he talked and Brandon marveled at the devastation.

"How many people missing?"

"Don't know yet. So many folks just passin' through, we might never know."

"Terrible."

"Sure is," the man agreed. "But I'm getting out while my luck holds. All this was rain down here in the valley, but it was all snow above the three-thousand-foot level I'm told."

"Winter gets an early start this far north," Brandon said, regretting the time they'd been delayed in Dyea, waiting for Conrad to heal. If they couldn't get down the Yukon before winter ended river travel, they might as well go back, too. Travel by sled with no dogs would be much more difficult, if not impossible, for two Cheechakos. And he didn't fancy sitting out the dark, cold months on the dreary Alaskan coast.

The stranger was true to his word. Brandon was able to buy beans, bacon, flour, axe, shovel, cooking utensils, and nearly everything they needed, including a tent, for $120. Both parties were satisfied with the arrangement, and Brandon congratulated himself that he had been up and out early enough to take advantage of this bargain, although he expected others would be selling out as well.

The man and his wife departed, hiking back down the trail the dozen miles to the coast, while Brandon split wood, shaving enough dry splinters to start a fire. He left his new tent standing where it was sheltering his newly purchased supplies on this spot of higher ground.

An hour later, Conrad was warming himself by the flames. The color had returned to his face. He still had spoken very little, and Brandon knew his partner was not yet fully recovered from his long ordeal and probably was in no condition to attack Chilkoot Pass. They would spend the rest of the day sorting and packing their new outfit, grateful to have replaced their lost goods so cheaply. While several of those flooded out were returning to Dyea, others, less affected, seemed determined to go on. Activity picked up, and shortly Brandon saw a trickle of Argonauts moving toward the Pass.

"We were lucky," Brandon said, handing his partner a tin plate of hash. The canned goods in their new outfit were varied and plentiful.

Conrad accepted the food without comment.

"We'll rest up and push on over the Pass tomorrow," Brandon continued. "Then it's all downhill to Lake Bennett, and we'll ride a boat the rest of the way. No more of this damned hiking and packing." He chattered on, trying to sound optimistic. He feared that Conrad was wavering, and didn't give his partner a chance to vent any negative feelings. "I wonder why storms and fires and floods always seem to happen in the middle of the night? I'm bushed. But if I keep moving, I'll make it the rest of the day. We need to get all this stuff packed in the right size bundles, so once we start, we can make several trips without having to stop and sort it."

Conrad drank the last of his coffee and got up. "I'll help. Where do I start?"

"Those tins of food are the heaviest, aside from the sacks of beans and flour," Brandon said, thankful that Conrad was apparently willing to give it another try. "Put it in stacks of about a hundred pounds each, and we'll see how much we've got."

Later that day, Brandon prepared another hot meal over their campfire, consisting of embalmed beef, boiled potatoes, and corn. Shortly after, Conrad sought his blankets while the sun was still above the trees.

Brandon sat alone for two more hours, staring into the dying flames and thinking of the days to come. He'd been too busy even to have any thoughts of home, but now he pictured Nellie Gentry and all of his friends in Louisville. No doubt they'd passed another dull day at their various jobs. He smiled to himself. A sense of satisfaction warmed his insides like a cup of hot soup. He had no desire to be anywhere but right here, right now. His earlier reservations about this adventure had vanished, and he eagerly looked forward to the coming days and weeks with a confidence he hadn't known in years.

CHAPTER
NINE

Each man worked like a demon,
as prow to rudder we raced;
The winds of the Wild cried, "Hurry!"
the voice of the waters, "Haste!"
. . . But what of the others that followed,
losing their boats by the score?
Well could we see them and hear them,
strung down that desolate shore.
Robert Service

Like a bright promise of future gold, the sun broke
clear of the morning clouds and flooded the valley with
welcome warmth and light. It revealed human activity
that would have done a colony of ants proud. Men were
salvaging and stacking the boards to begin rebuilding.
The sawmill was up and running, ripping new timber
into planks. Smoke rose from a dozen cooking fires and
out of the stovepipes of tents. New arrivals replaced the
discouraged and departed Argonauts. The village was
rising from its devastation like a mushroom in damp,
soggy ground.

"Eighteen miles to Lake Lindeman," Brandon said,
shrugging into his ninety-pound pack and adjusting the
tumpline across his forehead to take some of the strain.
"Let's go."

Conrad grinned. Food and sleep seemed to have restored Conrad to his old self, and the partners pulled out toward Chilkoot Pass with a spring in their step. The trail was rough, winding around and over gigantic granite boulders, climbing toward the base of the mountain. They hiked slowly, adjusting the loads now and then, picking their way carefully. Brandon had abandoned his rubber boots in favor of the high-top trail shoes he'd purchased in Seattle and had salvaged from the sled. They stopped frequently to catch their breath, sitting down and resting the packs on big rocks behind them. Brandon told himself he was taking it slower for the sake of Conrad's weakened condition, but, in truth, he was struggling as the pack grew heavier and heavier. They slipped and slid on mud and moss, leaning into their tumplines, grasping scrub pines and bushes to pull themselves upward. Where the trail skirted the river, they had to place one foot ahead of the other on a narrow ledge, not daring to look down into the rushing torrent below.

"Gawdammit, if you're not gonna climb, get outta the way!" a burly hiker rasped breathlessly when they stopped short in front of him to rest. They pulled off the trail at a wider point, and the line surged forward. But others were dropping out of the queue as well, men and women alike, weaker than the two partners, women dressed in inappropriate long skirts and city shoes. The two men heaved up their packs and started on. Two hundred feet, six hundred feet . . . Brandon's leg muscles were aching with every step now. Never had he been taxed to this extreme. In spite of the chilly air, sweat trickled down his face. Maybe they should have started with forty-pound packs. Moaning, crying, gasping hikers lay prone alongside the trail every few yards. The god of the mountain was exacting his toll.

"Hey, mister, how far to the top?" Brandon hailed a returning hiker.

"How many pounds you got on your back?"

"Ninety."

"Then it's about nine hundred miles."

"*How* far?" a woman behind Brandon asked, her nostrils flaring.

"Without a pack, it's a mile and a half." He smiled at the unburdened woman.

By ten o'clock they reached a place dubbed Stonehouse. It was only a resting point where a huge, overhanging boulder jutted out of the mountainside and served as a last place to rest before the assault on the final half-mile climb that spiked upward at a forty-five-degree angle. Brandon squinted up the winding trail where it disappeared in fog and mist near the summit. The wind and sun had begun to shred and dissipate the fog, and he saw that the upper part of the Pass was covered with snow. Back-tripping hikers passing by advised them that the scales were located just this side of the summit where all goods had to be weighed for Canadian customs.

Just as they lifted their loads and trudged on, Brandon in the lead, a south wind began to blow up the cañon. It helped push them along, but it was also softening the snow above, turning it into slush, and making the trail even slicker. Brandon almost wished the trail had been covered in snow as they got in line and started upward. Steps cut into snow and ice would have been easier than the sharp rocks.

Trudging mechanically, heads down, they finally reached the scales and unloaded their packs. Then it was off downhill at a trot for another load. Brandon had no fear of thievery since packs and boxes of perfectly good articles had been abandoned all along the trail and were there for anyone to pick up.

Without pausing for food, they made two more trips that day, carrying a total of five hundred and eighty pounds. It took two and a half hours just for the round trip of three miles from Sheep Camp to Stonehouse.

That night they slept like dead men in their tent at Sheep Camp. The next morning after a breakfast of flapjacks, maple syrup, bacon, and coffee, they started again, gradually stretching out and limbering up their aching legs and back muscles.

The trail was lined with carts and sleds drawn by horses, dogs, oxen, and mules. One man from Seattle even had an elk pulling his load. As they paused for breath that afternoon near Stonehouse, Brandon noted the sun striking a glacier some distance to the left of the trail. The pale green mass of ice seemed to overhang the mountain. Even as he looked, a report like a distant cannon reached his ears. The face of the glacier burst apart, and millions of tons of ice came crashing down the mountainside with a roar like thunder. A great cloud of dust billowed into the air as tons of ice cascaded down and slid to rest in the valley below.

"Damn!" Conrad breathed.

They looked at each other. This awesome display of nature's power made Brandon feel even smaller as they took up their packs and started again. He regretted having lost his camera and film in the flood; his friends at home would never believe the size and majesty of this country without some visual record.

A few minutes later they caught up to an older man struggling along with an oversize pack. A woman and a little girl trailed behind him. He turned a despairing face to Brandon as the pair passed by. "God Almighty keeps his gold in a mighty safe place, don't He?"

They all burst into laughter, and it seemed to lighten the load. It was a good feeling to know they were all in this together.

Before they quit, exhausted, they had hauled another six hundred twenty-one pounds to the scales. By now, repeated trips had taught them the best routes, the easiest steps, and the best resting places.

Brandon was thankful a flood did not occur that night because they both slept like two sticks of cordwood. The third and fourth days were a repeat of the first two, except that their bodies were becoming lean, their leg muscles hardened to the trail. In spite of the severe toil, even Conrad's ribs seemed to be healing. Their bellies grew flatter, their faces leaner. But, to add to their miseries, they both contracted diarrhea. Others at Sheep Camp had the same problem, and they laid the cause to the river water that was polluted by the carcasses of dead horses. Brandon took to straining and boiling their water, and the condition disappeared the next day, leaving them weak, but well. The fifth and sixth days they got the entire load of 2,500 pounds from the scales to the summit of Chilkoot Pass. There, Canadian Mounted Police had set up headquarters in a small log cabin and a large open tent to collect duty on the outfits entering their country.

Hundreds of tons of goods were piled everywhere in the foot-deep snow that blanketed the summit. After asking the other Argonauts who were waiting their turn, Brandon discovered they would be required to produce bills for the total weight of their goods. They had 2,500 pounds of supplies, but receipts for only 1,900 pounds.

"Mister, I tell ya how it worked for a friend of mine," a bearded man in line by the custom broker's tent said to Brandon when he overheard their plight. "Slip a five-dollar note between the bills when you go in to the broker. He'll certify you got proof of all twenty-five hundred pounds of your load."

"I heard the Mounties couldn't be bribed."

"Apparently that don't apply to all of them."

"Don't they require a ton of supplies for each man?"

"Supposed to. But just look at all this . . ." He waved his arm at the milling crowd and the piles of bales heaped everywhere. "How the hell are three or four Mounties gonna check hundreds of tons of stuff? Just have your partner wander off somewhere. For all they know, you're by yourself."

Brandon did as he was advised, and the customs broker, bundled up in furs, pocketed the five dollars, never questioning the bills presented to him. Then Brandon got into another queue to the log cabin and, an hour later, paid $43.50 duty, and received his receipt. No attempt was made to inspect the goods.

Brandon felt they had passed a major hurdle, as he came out of the cabin grinning and waving the receipt at Conrad.

"It's getting pretty late in the day to start down. You want to see if we can camp here and get a fresh start in the morning?" Brandon asked, seeing the pale face of his friend, pinched with cold and fatigue. "I'm tired," he added, so Conrad would not think he was being pitied.

"Camp out in the snow?"

"No. Some enterprising soul has thrown up a bunkhouse over yonder. It's not much, but it's shelter."

"Fine by me."

The bunkhouse was a board affair with a canvas roof and wooden bunks — no blankets furnished. Brandon paid their fifty cents each for the bunks and seventy-five each for a supper of ham, eggs, and beans. Strength restored by the food, they went to the log hut and chatted with the Mounted Police who had finished their work for the day. In the course of the conversation, Brandon found out the Mounties were short of food and arranged to sell them two hundred pounds of potatoes at ten cents a pound.

"An extra twenty dollars will come in handy," Brandon told Conrad at nine o'clock that evening as they trudged through the snow to the flimsy bunkhouse. "I'm glad you were taking a rough inventory while I was standing in those lines earlier. We have more spuds than we need and that's two hundred pounds we won't have to carry any farther."

They spent a miserable night. Brandon had hoped they'd both get some much-needed sleep. They were sorely disappointed. Even though each of them dug a blanket out of their gear and lay down in all their clothes on the hard bunk, they were chilled in the unheated structure. Brandon's socks were wet, but he dared not take off his boots for fear his feet would freeze. Several times he got up in the darkness and stamped the numbness out of his feet until he again felt the prickly warmth of blood in his toes. He looked toward the still form of Conrad in the other bunk, wondering if he were asleep or was just shivering under the blanket, wishing for an early dawn.

After an eternity, they were up by the first rays of the sun, drinking coffee and eating flapjacks. The hot food and the warming sun gave them renewed strength as they began packing their loads downhill, out of the melting snow to the lower elevations. A string of glacial lakes — Crater Lake, Long Lake, and Deep Lake — led several miles to Lake Lindeman where they could navigate by water all the way to Dawson.

Hiking down the other side, at first a relief soon became an agony, their thigh muscles braking the weight on steep inclines. They quickly learned that carrying loads downhill on loose shale was nearly as difficult as climbing. They slipped and slid, bruising their shins, gouging their boots.

When he had time to look, now and then pausing to take a breather, Brandon was thrilled by the panorama opening up before them. A vast sweep of mountain valley stretched out below their feet. He could see the first two lakes in the distance — Crater Lake and Long Lake. Deep Lake lay just beyond his vision. Their goal was the next lake in the chain — Lake Lindeman — where they would stop and somehow construct a boat to take them the rest of the way. Focusing on that goal made the pain in his legs and feet endurable. Only a few more miles, he thought. As he shifted his shoulders in a pack that weighed like a boulder on his back, he purposely ignored the thought of having to backtrack several times between the summit and Lake Lindeman to get their entire outfit down along this trail to the lakeshore. He wished the lakes were navigable beginning with Crater Lake, to save several miles of packing. But it was not to be. Maybe these extra miles would be the stumbling block that would discourage a few dozen more stampeders who lacked his own grim determination — anything to whittle down the competition.

He inhaled deeply and continued down the trail, his eyes on the rough, winding path ahead where each painful step brought him closer to the golden dust that he hoped would ensure his future. He would have welcomed enough snow to use the long sled. But the few stretches of snow and ice only served to make footing treacherous. Loose rocks and patches of melting snow underfoot threatened to spill them at the first unwary step. During the first two hours of this, they counted a half dozen hikers crashing and tumbling down the talus slope, cursing the ill luck of ankle and knee injuries and cuts and bruises from the sharp rocks.

Brandon discovered the fifteen miles from Chilkoot Pass to Lake Lindeman was pure torture. For the first few miles, he led the way, constantly watching Conrad over his shoulder. The weight of his own pack grew heavier, his legs shakier. It was really as much for himself as for Conrad that he stopped after seven miles. Some enterprising Argonaut had thrown up a cabin as a makeshift eating place. For two dollars each, they enjoyed an early supper of bean soup, ham and eggs of uncertain age, prunes, bread and butter.

"Sorry about that bread, gents," the proprietor said. "I was in too much of a hurry, and it's a might doughy in the middle."

Brandon ate it anyway.

"How much farther to Lake Lindeman?" Conrad asked the man.

"About seven miles."

Conrad swallowed the last of his coffee and turned to Brandon. "Think we can make it by dark?"

Wishing with all his heart he could drop down where he sat and sleep for two days, Brandon replied: "Sure. No problem. We'll camp there and start back for the next load first thing in the morning."

The last two miles to Lindeman in the lingering Arctic twilight were grueling. The trail led through a scrub pine forest where they tripped on roots curled around the rocks and boulders. Brandon felt as if his legs were half wood and half rubber as he stumbled along. He had switched from his lacerated rubber boots

109

to his trail shoes, but the sharp rocks gashed the leather as well. Conrad uttered no complaints, but doggedly trudged on, head down, his labored breath *whooshing* from his lungs at every jarring step.

A tiny village had sprung up along the lakeshore, but the two men selected a level campsite away from hundreds of others and pitched the white tent Conrad was packing. More exhausted than hungry, both men went to bed without supper.

Brandon was up in the early light and had a fire going. They ate a huge breakfast of bacon, beans, flapjacks, and coffee before starting on the back trail, carrying their empty pack frames made of willow.

It took a mile or two to work the stiffness out of their limbs and muscles. In spite of their boots and shoes being cut and scarred, they always took pains to keep their feet dry and free from blisters, changing their socks overnight and bathing their feet in cold lake water, then rubbing them with alcohol. "Toughens the skin," Brandon said. "And, to avoid chaffing, be careful there are no wrinkles in your socks."

Since their two-wheeled cart had been washed away, and no packers were available for hire — even if they'd had the money — they managed to make two round trips that day, leaving about half their goods still on the summit.

"By God, I think I'm going to make this, after all," Conrad said the second morning as he squatted by the campfire and filled his tin plate.

"It'll either kill you or make a man of you," Brandon answered. "How're the ribs?"

"I think all that exercise has helped heal them."

Brandon grinned. "I've got some more good news. Before you were up, I walked down the shore a ways to wash and get some water in the coffee pot. Found a big Norwegian named Sjolseth. He and his two sons are building and selling boats. They look like they know what they're about. Somebody had backed out on a boat they had almost finished, and I told him we wanted it. Didn't figure you and I had the time or energy or know-how to build our own."

"We got any money left?" Conrad asked.

"Some. I gave them our six-foot crosscut saw as a down payment. They want another hundred and twenty for a twenty-four foot boat with mast, sails, and oars."

Conrad arched his eyebrows in silent query.

"I know. It's a pretty steep price, but what other choice have we got? We don't have that much money, but I think maybe when the boat is done, I can wangle some kind of arrangement. After all, his first buyer has already backed out on him. He'll be eager to get rid of it. A lot of stampeders are building their own boats and scows. I don't think the demand is all that great."

Conrad looked dubious, but made no reply.

"If we need more cash, we can always sell some of those sacks of dried beans. We got enough to feed a battalion, and I'd rather leave a few sacks at Chilkoot than pack 'em all the way down here."

"We can't be getting rid of too much of our food, no matter how much it weighs."

"Right you are," Brandon agreed. "And I think three more hard days will get all our stuff down here. By that time, our boat should be ready." He looked off along the shore where several parties were laboriously sawing planks from logs on raised platforms they had erected. "Talk about heartbreaking work!" he said. "No saw pits for me! I tried that once to help a friend who was building a house from timber on his land. Wanted to do it all himself without hiring a mill to cut the lumber. One man above and one below pushing and pulling that damned saw. It was hell! The saw blade binds in that green wood, sawdust falls into your eyes, it's tough to keep the blade on a straight, chalked line. But the worst thing is the ache in the arms and shoulders. You think packing is hard work? It pales by comparison. And your lungs nearly bust, too."

Even as he spoke, they heard loud cursing and shouting. A man jumped down from the top of a log frame and lunged at the man on the saw handle below. The two locked together, one getting a choke hold as they fell, rolling on the ground.

"See what I mean?"

Three mornings later Brandon opened his eyes and looked up at the overhead white canvas. Stretching his stiff muscles he felt a great deal of satisfaction that all of their supplies finally surrounded them. Coming fully awake, he also realized that he hadn't the slightest idea what day it was. Not only was he ignorant of the day of the week, he could only guess from the skim of ice on a nearby water bucket that it was past the first week of October. When he threw back the tent flap and looked out to a glorious, sunny morning, he noted that the snow line had crept down a little lower on the distant mountains.

"'Old time is yet a-flying. The flowers that bloom today tomorrow will be dying,'" he quoted aloud to himself. Was that scrap of poetry by Robert Herrick or John Donne? He couldn't remember. But when he drew in a deep breath, the frosty air told him better than any poem what was nearly upon them.

He glanced at the flat lake. It was past time for flowers. In fact, the freeze-up was rushing to lock up the navigation downriver to Dawson. They would have to hurry.

"Up and at 'em," he greeted a sleepy-eyed Conrad. "Time to get our boat from Sjolseth." He grinned. "Enough of this exercise. We're riding the rest of the way."

"Forget breakfast," Conrad said, pulling on his boots. "We can eat later. Let's get that boat and get loaded."

Brandon nodded, looking out at the dozens of other men packing gear up and down the open shoreline and several boats already far out on the lake, oars dipping and flashing in the morning sun.

They walked the half mile to the Sjolseth boat-building enterprise. The two sons were boiling green boards preparatory to bending them around several framed hulls that rested upside-down on blocks.

The paternal brown-bearded Sjolseth was working with the sleeves of his flannel shirt rolled up past the elbows. He looked up from smoothing a gunwale and shook the curls of shavings from his plane. "There she be," he said, standing up with a grunt.

"That the one?"

"Yep. Rough, but sturdy. No paint, of course."

Brandon walked around and inspected the boat. How a man could build such a beautiful hull under such primitive conditions was a mystery to him. Some people just had the knack. He was certain this man and his sons were experienced — probably professional — boat builders. He tried not to show his enthusiasm for the graceful sheer, the deep bow, and the heavy pine construction of the vessel.

"Looks good," was all he said, nodding approvingly.

"A six-inch keel runs along the bottom from amidships," Sjolseth said. "That'll keep 'er going to windward pretty good."

"She won't point too well with that square sail," Brandon countered.

"Oh, you can rig that as a lateen sail, or even a fore-and-after," the bearded man said. "Any way you want to use it." He was obviously proud of his work. "Worth even more than the hundred fifty I'm charging for it," he said.

"I thought you quoted me a hundred twenty the other day, less about fifteen for that new saw I gave you," Brandon said.

The big Norwegian's face clouded. "You must be mistaken. "Maybe a flat scow you could get for a hundred, but not this beauty."

In spite of the fact the boat was made of unpainted green lumber and the seams were oozing oakum and pitch, it was obviously the product of skilled hands.

114

"I'll give you eighty, plus a hundred pounds of potatoes," Brandon offered quickly, thinking they could do without the remaining spuds which hadn't been sold to the Mounted Police.

"Huh! What do I need of more food? We do not plan to spend the winter in this country. We are here to make money, my sons and I." He was no longer the friendly, jovial boat builder. He had become the hard, no-nonsense businessman. "If you don't want my boat, there are others here who do . . . and will pay my price." He waved a dismissal. "We have no time to dicker. Either pay and take the boat, or be gone. I must get on with my work. The freeze-up comes soon."

"Offer him my Marlin," Conrad urged in an undertone.

Brandon shook his head. "That's more necessary than the boat."

"Then forget about him and his boat," Conrad muttered, obviously not used to begging or bartering. "We'll catch a ride downriver with some other party."

"Word is, there are bad rapids. I've had enough experience boating that I don't want to trust myself to some stranger and his home-made craft that could get us drowned or all our food and gear lost."

Ingemar Sjolseth had already turned away and was dragging some freshly sawn boards to a growing stack nearby.

"Looks like I came along at just the right time," a male voice interrupted.

Brandon turned and his throat constricted as he saw George and Annie O'Connell standing a few feet away.

CHAPTER
TEN

The river springs like a racer,
sweeps through a gash in the rock;
Butts at the boulder-ribbed bottom,
staggers and rears at the shock;
Leaps like a terrified monster,
writhes in its fury and pain;
Then with the crash of a demon
springs to the onset again.
Robert Service

The O'Connells had obviously overheard the exchange with the bearded Norwegian. The white-haired lawyer was dressed in a striped, collarless shirt and blue denim pants. "You look vaguely familiar," O'Connell said, staring at Brandon. "Have we met somewhere before?"

He was so drunk he doesn't remember, Brandon thought, quickly deciding not to enlighten him, at least for the moment. "I don't think so," he replied, then threw a sharp glance at Annie who was gazing at him. She gave a barely perceptible shake of her head.

O'Connell pulled a gold money clip from his pocket and began peeling greenbacks from a thick wad. "Here's the hundred and fifty you need," he said, holding out the money to Brandon. "Buy that boat and let's be on our way."

116

Brandon stared, open-mouthed. Before he could say anything, Annie blurted out: "We had some problems with our party, and have split off from them. My husband thought maybe we could join the two of you."

"Especially since you seem to be somewhat impecunious at the moment." The lawyer smiled deprecatingly. "All four of us can get down the river with no further delay." He appeared to think his bankroll now put him in charge. "Come on!" O'Connell urged impatiently. "Hey, you!" He turned to yell at Sjolseth. "Here's your money. He wants that boat."

Brandon's second impression of O'Connell was little better than the first, and he had to clamp his mouth shut to keep from making a sharp retort. It was not hard to imagine how the man's grating, overbearing attitude had led to trouble. It was probably due only to the peacekeeping efforts of Annie that the couple had come this far with their traveling party before being ostracized.

With a curious look at Brandon, the Norwegian came over and took the bills, flipping the edges for a quick count. "There she is," he said shortly, jerking a thumb at the boat and stuffing the bills into his side pocket. Then he fished some folded paper and a pencil from the pocket in the bib of his overalls. Squatting, he smoothed the paper across his knee and laboriously signed it, his big, callused fingers dwarfing the pencil. "Bill of sale." He handed Brandon two sheets of paper.

"Annie, get our stuff and start loading up," George said over his shoulder to the woman behind him. "We'll be off within the hour. I'm sure these gentlemen don't mind. Looks like we can help each other out." He smiled ingratiatingly.

"Who're you?" Conrad asked, looking none too pleased with this turn of events.

O'Connell introduced himself and his wife, who merely nodded without offering her hand or speaking. She was not as ornately dressed as when Brandon had last seen her on the riverboat, but she still wore a long skirt and a short jacket over a frilly blouse. Her only concession to the wilderness was a broad-brimmed hat and some sort of wedge-heeled, lace-up boots.

Brandon's thoughts were racing. Except for a couple of Soapy Smith's boys, these two were probably the last people he wanted to spend the next couple of weeks with in a boat or camp. "Excuse me a moment while I talk to my partner," Brandon said, motioning Conrad aside.

When he briefly explained how he happened to know the O'Connells, the furrow between Conrad's eyes deepened. "Forget this idea. We'd be better off taking our chances with somebody else."

"As long as he doesn't remember me, I think it will be all right," Brandon said. "The only thing these two know about packing they must have learned thus far on the trail. I seriously doubt they have any experience boating. It's a good bet George made an ass of himself and maybe some serious enemies, so their party cut them loose. I think I can manage him as long as he's sober."

"I don't think he's sober at the moment. If he likes the sauce that much, probably half his duffel is booze."

"You may be right, but if we want to get down the lakes and rivers before freeze-up, we have to act now. I

118

say we give it a shot. If it doesn't work, we can get rid of them when we reach Dawson. After all" — he glanced at the twenty-two-foot boat setting at the water's edge — "he actually owns that boat now, and could just as easily put his wife in it without us and sail off."

"A middle-aged city lawyer with no experience . . . ," Conrad began.

"Exactly. That's the only reason you and I are even in the picture."

Conrad blew out his cheeks in a long breath, shrugged, and nodded his head in resignation. "Let's get going, then."

By ten o'clock, Brandon and Conrad were shoving the loaded boat into the lake. Even though the stern rested in the water, it was a struggle to get the heavy vessel afloat. After a minute or two of strain, they called on George O'Connell to help. Even Annie, with her high-top boots and long skirt, sloshed out into the cold water, adding what she could to the effort.

When the boat finally floated free, they all tumbled over the sides on top of the gear, and a spontaneous cheer went up from Brandon, Conrad, and Annie. George was cursing his wet shoes.

The partners settled themselves at the oars and rowed the craft out into deeper water before trying to raise the sail.

"I hereby christen this boat *Cincy*," George said, wringing out his socks onto the port gunwale. "After my hometown."

Brandon didn't care if the boat had a name, but said over his shoulder: "To properly christen it, you'll have to bust a bottle over the bow."

"And waste a good bottle of brandy? You're out of your mind!" the lawyer retorted.

The O'Connells' gear and food consisted of less than a fourth of what the partners were packing. Brandon wondered how they expected to survive the winter in the interior on that small amount of grub and clothing. Then it struck him that O'Connell probably figured to buy whatever he needed from unlucky or discouraged stampeders.

Conrad confided to Brandon that, even though he owned a yacht on the Chesapeake, he had limited sailing experience and usually left the crewing of the large ketch to hired sailors while he entertained the guests. That left Brandon as the only one of the quartet who had any practical small boat experience.

Lake Lindeman was nearly flat calm, for which Brandon was grateful as he untangled the lines and figured out how the square sail worked. It was a rather crude arrangement Sjolseth had rigged. The sail was made from canvas sacks sewn together. As long as the breeze was at their backs, it would be effective. Brandon wasn't so sure how well the sail would drive them to windward.

He secured the halyard, then settled himself at the tiller. At first the only breeze was a light stirring of air from the northwest. But, as the sun rose higher and the air warmed, a westerly wind sprang up, coming at them from the port side. With four adults and more than a

120

ton of goods, the boat had all the buoyancy of a water-logged tree trunk. According to the map, Lake Lindeman was only about six miles long. The wind was not coming down the long fetch of the lake, so its force was broken by the hills of the nearby shore and did not kick up waves of any size. Even so, Brandon instructed the other three to move to the port side of the boat to balance the weight. It took Brandon about a half hour to get the feel of the new craft so he was able to judge how it reacted to the rudder.

The boat began to heel to the freshening breeze, and Brandon was impressed at how quickly the wind could get up on this Northern lake. The starboard gunwale dipped perilously close to the water's edge. He held the end of the mainsheet in one hand, having given it a turn around a thwart to take the pressure off his arm. The water became choppy, and the boat began to roll as it surged ahead. He held it to a fine edge, gauging the wind on his cheek and the feel of the pressure on the rudder. Water licked along the gunwale, slopping over into the boat.

"Watch out!" O'Connell cried, cringing back to the high side. Another dollop of water splashed over the side. "Dammit! I said be careful. You're going to capsize us!"

Brandon spilled some of the air from the sail, and the boat straightened up. The six-inch keel kept the boat from sliding sideways to any great degree, and the load was good ballast for maintaining a low center of gravity. Brandon was grateful to the bluff Norwegian for building heavy and giving the vessel a deep hull. They needed every inch of freeboard they had, and then some.

"What's wrong with you, man?" O'Connell snapped, looking unusually pale in the morning sun. "Quit making us lean so far over."

"We've got to make time. We have a long way to go," Brandon said, letting his eyes rove from the belly of the home-made sail to the water foaming alongside.

The lawyer's eyes were wide with fear, even as he kept up his bluster. Brandon took a savage delight in the discomfort of the man. Fear of being thrown into an icy lake couldn't be as bad as facing the muzzle of a loaded Derringer, he thought. Brandon had smelled alcohol on the lawyer this morning. Either the man was an habitual drunk who nipped at breakfast, or he was having a little hair of the dog to ease the pain of a hangover. Brandon smiled grimly to himself as he hauled in on the sheet, and the boat responded by heeling dangerously. O'Connell leaned over the high side of his *Cincy* and retched. The boat rolled down into a wave, and cold spray burst over the windward side, drenching George O'Connell and throwing a finer mist over everyone else.

Annie O'Connell and Conrad were silently hanging on, averting their faces from the wind and spray. Annie was a good sport. Brandon couldn't keep his eyes off her. She appeared to have cut her hair since he first saw her. It was barely collar-length now, and she pulled off her hat, letting her black tresses blow, seeming to glory in the thrilling ride, laughing at the fine spray that was blown over the weather side. She ignored her husband, offering him no comfort in his distress. A strange couple, Brandon thought. Either an unhappy marriage, or one that had reached a level of compromise.

The wind gusted from the west-northwest and drove the deeply laden boat along. With each hour, Brandon gained more and more confidence. They were passed by four smaller, lighter boats and, in turn, overtook a large scow and two boats whose occupants apparently didn't have the slightest skill at seamanship. Three boats had only oars and no sails. As the *Cincy* tore past them, the sweating rowers looked up with anguished, envious faces.

If only the wind and weather would stay fair for another week or so, Brandon thought, the four of them could make the Yukon River and Dawson. Maybe the gods were at last smiling on them after all the hardships and ill luck they'd experienced.

The wind steadied in velocity and direction, and they made the foot of Lake Lindeman by early afternoon. Tents lined a quarter-mile strip where stampeders ahead of them had paused to rest and assess their next hazard, a rocky channel sucking out the lower end of the lake. Known as One-Mile Rapids, it connected Lindeman to Lake Bennett.

Brandon drove the boat shoreward. They all needed to stretch their legs, and Annie had let him know in a whisper that she had to heed a call of nature. The bow grated on the rocky beach, and Conrad quickly dropped the sail. Brandon leaped out and secured the painter of the boat to a rock, then gave his hand to Annie who debarked barefoot, holding her wet shoes in the other hand. Her husband had gone on ahead without waiting for her. Curious, Brandon looked after him and saw George take a surreptitious gulp from a pocket flask. Annie thanked Brandon with her eyes for his courtesy, then hurried after her husband.

"Better be careful how you deal with her," Conrad said, noticing the interplay. "If he's so jealous of her that he'd take a shot at you in front of witnesses, he'd sure as hell do it again, whether he remembers you or not. Especially if he's liquored up."

"I know. I wonder why she sticks with him?" Brandon muttered.

"Maybe she likes what his money can buy," Conrad said. "I've seen wives among my circle of well-off acquaintances do the very same."

"What about a woman's self-respect?"

Conrad shrugged. "You make your choices and you live with them. Life is all about compromises and trade-offs, even for the wealthy." He bent to straighten out the piled sail and the tangled halyard in the bottom of the boat.

Then the two men walked down toward the chute that funneled out the lower end of the lake. They relieved themselves behind a boulder, then watched a double-ended boat descend into the maëlstrom. There were two men in it — one in the bow and the other at the steering sweep. It plunged out of sight behind a standing wave, then came up, streaming water like a leaping whale before slamming back into the water. The man in the stern was leaning hard on the sweep when it suddenly came loose from its pivot, and the boat spun sideways in the current. Brandon could sense their panic as they lost control, and the boat headed for a boulder in midstream twenty yards below. It slammed sideways into the boulder, careened off, and disappeared around a bend.

Brandon and Conrad looked at each other, then quickly away, neither voicing his thoughts. They walked silently back to the *Cincy*.

"Think we ought to portage?" Conrad said when they reached their boat and saw the O'Connells approaching in the distance.

Brandon didn't reply for several seconds. He'd had no experience running white water, but wasn't about to let anyone else know. Succeed or fail, he would be experienced before the hour was out. The fate of their entire venture lay in his hands. It was his decision.

"We're sure to ship some water if we don't portage some of this stuff," Conrad continued.

"No portaging," Brandon said firmly. "I've carried my last load for now. Besides, we haven't got time. We're running too many days behind as it is. We'll shift some of the cargo to trim the balance a little, and I'll use the two of them for shifting ballast. You'll guide me from the bow, and I'll take the extra steering sweep back here so it'll be handy if I need it in a hurry. We can run through. It's only a mile long."

"You think that's wise?" Conrad asked quietly.

"We didn't come up here to play it safe. If others ahead have done it, we can, too. This is a good, stable boat. Miles Cañon and White Horse Cañon farther down are a lot worse, I'm told. If we're going to cave in at the first sign of rough water, we might as well go home." He pointed. "Fold that sail and spread it over the bow to ward off most of the spray we'll be taking forward."

Brandon untied the painter as George and Annie walked up. "We'll be camping on the lower end of Lake Bennett before supper time," he said confidently. "Cast off." He hoped he sounded more convincing than he felt.

CHAPTER
ELEVEN

Beneath us the green tumult churning,
above us the cavernous gloom;
Around us, swift twisting and turning,
the black, sullen walls of a tomb . . .
Then, like a rumble of thunder,
heard we a canorous roar.
Leaping and boiling and seething,
saw we a cauldron afume;
There was the rage of the rapids,
there was the menace of doom.
Robert Service

His feet braced, Brandon threw his weight against the steering oar. The boat's heading barely changed as the vessel plunged ahead in the grip of the current. A roar drowned every sound. He squinted ahead through stinging spray at Conrad who knelt in the bow, giving him hand signals. White water boiled on both sides of the boat, and several gallons came over the side as the bow veered suddenly. Brandon straightened it up just in time to see Conrad frantically signaling him to bear to starboard. A jutting rock in mid-stream had killed a raft, and its upended, splintered remnants screamed a silent warning. Brandon pulled hard on the sweep, thankful he had the leverage of the long, thick oar. They shot past the boulder at express-train speed, clearing it by a bare six feet.

The *Cincy* bucked and wallowed drunkenly for the next several hundred yards as the stream dropped over the glacial boulders, until finally over the last quarter mile the river began to smooth out as the heavy boat was spun into quieter water. Brandon's muscles were tense, and he was soaked with sweat and spray, his heart pounding. He tried to conceal the fact that his legs were shaking as he seated himself in the stern. The worst was over; they'd made it without a portage, bringing the overloaded boat safely through.

"Wahooo!" A shout of elation burst from his throat, releasing the tension. He had done it! A little skill and a lot of nerve and good luck had seen him through.

Conrad jerked his head around with a look of alarm, and the O'Connells stared at Brandon as if he'd gone mad.

"What a ride!" Brandon yelled.

Conrad showed a gap-toothed grin and gave him the thumbs-up sign.

"Grab that bucket and start bailing," Brandon ordered when he saw a pale George O'Connell looking at him. Several inches of water were sloshing around their feet. They'd made an effort to get most of the perishables, such as the beans and flour, on top of the pile, but he suspected some of it had probably still been ruined.

With a degree of satisfaction, Brandon saw Lake Bennett spreading before them in the distance. Miles Cañon and White Horse Rapids, which were reputed to be much worse than One-Mile Rapids, still lay downstream. But he would deal with them in their turn. Nothing would spoil this moment.

They floated around the last bend in the stream and came in sight of the tent city of Bennett that had sprung up where the White Pass Trail and the Chilkoot Pass Trail converged. The whine and screech of a sawmill ripping logs and the staccato rapping of hammers were the first sounds that rent the quiet. The aroma of fresh-cut spruce was in the air. Even though someone had erected a steam-powered sawmill, Brandon assumed they were charging high prices for their finished lumber since eight or ten saw pits were in full operation, the men struggling to cut their own logs with two-man crosscut saws. Men and women hurried back and forth, some striking tents, some cooking, some loading boats or talking in small groups. The lakeshore was lined with boats, rafts, and flat-bottomed, blunt-ended scows.

"Like squirrels getting ready for winter," Brandon said to Conrad, waving at all the activity. He breathed deeply, savoring the smell of wood smoke and cooking food.

The red coat of a policeman caught his eye as the Mountie moved among the dark clothing of the Argonauts. Skeletal white ribs of inverted boats under construction were propped up here and there.

As the stream debouched into Lake Bennett, Brandon took advantage of the dying current to guide the boat to shore. He was reluctant to stop, but Conrad reminded him the inspector at Chilkoot Pass had said Bennett was where all boats had to be registered.

The operation was quick. Barely twenty minutes later, the number 1,952 was burned into each side of the *Cincy*'s bow with a hot iron.

"There you are, gentlemen . . . and lady," the young Mountie said, stepping back and replacing the last smoking branding iron in a bucket of hot coals.

"Besides making money for the Canadian government, what purpose does *that* serve?" George O'Connell grumbled.

"As you can see, one thousand nine hundred and fifty-one boats have already passed here ahead of you," was the Mountie's cheerful response. "I'll need to record your names with this number. It allows us to keep track of all the vessels going down, if we ever have to go looking for anyone lost or in trouble."

O'Connell grunted but said nothing.

"By the way, I'll need to see your receipt for the timber you cut to make this boat."

"There's a charge for that, too?" Conrad asked.

"We didn't build this boat, but here's the receipt from the man who did," Brandon said, digging into his side pants pocket and producing some damp, creased papers. "I never really looked at it."

The policeman examined the slips of paper. "OK, one of these is your receipt for the boat and the other is a copy of the builder's receipt for two hundred and fifty board feet of timber. The fee's been paid." He handed the papers back. "There will be a fee of ten dollars for

130

each one in your party to purchase a miner's license," the Mountie continued.

"A *miner's license?*" O'Connell burst out. "What kind of bureaucratic crap is this?"

The Mountie shot him a sharp look, and Annie tugged at her husband's arm and said something under her breath.

"This license grants each of you the privilege for one year to mine, hunt, fish, and cut timber for your own use only . . . not for commercial purposes."

"Hell, I thought we were coming to a damned wilderness!" O'Connell grated, his bloodshot eyes glaring from beneath disheveled white hair. "Now here we are being taxed to death before we even see the first damned speck of gold."

"A very minimal tax, considering the riches that are being taken out of this country by outsiders," the Mountie replied evenly, his ruddy cheeks giving the only hint of his irritation.

"George, please," Annie said, "this policeman is only doing his job."

"Legal fleecing," the lawyer said, shaking off his wife, apparently determined to have the last word. "There was nothing but a bunch of dirty Indians in this so-called 'country' before all these good people came up here from the States to give it some kind of civilizing influence. I guess the Queen, or the government in Ottawa, saw a good chance to fill their coffers at our expense."

The young Mountie looked carefully at O'Connell. "Have you been drinking, sir? Any more backtalk and

I'll arrest you for public intoxication and creating a disturbance. The fine for that will be considerably more than these license fees."

Brandon suddenly had an urge to prod the lawyer to further outbursts so he would be arrested. A convenient excuse for leaving him behind; then he and Conrad could be rid of the O'Connells. But Annie finally drew her husband away while Brandon hurriedly purchased miners' licenses for all four of them.

With a quick glance at the high, cirrus clouds sliding across the blue sky, Brandon hustled them all back into the boat and shoved off. Conrad rowed out about fifty yards to where cat's-paws were marring the flat surface of the lake, just beyond where the wind was being blocked by the mountain behind them. Then he hoisted the sail, and the *Cincy* caught the faint breeze, and they were off. Conrad rigged a handheld fishing line, baited with a lure he'd made from a feather. In less than thirty minutes of trolling, he snagged a three-pound trout that he placed in a bucket of water.

"A good omen," Brandon said, eyeing the fish. "Twenty-four miles to the lower end of this lake," he added, uncapping a canteen and taking a swallow of water. "We should be there before dark."

The long lake lay mostly in a north-south direction. During the long afternoon's sail, Brandon had no sense of being in a wilderness, for he once counted seventy-six boats of various kinds in sight at one time. There was no telling how many more were in this vast flotilla that stretched out of sight ahead and behind them. The wind continued to increase, gusting from

132

one direction and then another, requiring constant vigilance as they were backwinded several times.

Brandon watched as several boaters, shouting and waving challenges at one other, began to race. In the space of an hour, he saw one broach and capsize; another split its sail from top to bottom. A third held onto its flattened sail too long and drove itself right under. One moment the plunging craft was there, and the next it was gone in the trough between two waves. Brandon stared hard across a hundred yards of wild water, but the boat didn't reappear. One surge of water passed, then another, and a succession of green, feather-edged waves continued to roll, uninterrupted, with no sign of the boat or its occupants.

Brandon let out the breath he'd been holding. "By God! Pitchpoled and gone," he breathed, feeling a chill go up his back. The boat was wood, but its heavy load was lashed down and had apparently carried the craft and its men to the bottom. Brandon turned his attention back to his own craft and spilled some of the heavy wind from the sail to give him more control.

The wind held steady on their port beam, and the boat surged along. By now he'd mastered the trick of keeping the *Cincy* on its fastest point of sailing without excessive heel. Everything in the boat remained dry. He gloried in this quick mode of transport. As the rocky, forested shoreline moved steadily past, he recalled the pain of packing their gear endless miles. Now it was a downhill ride all the way to Dawson.

The gentle rocking motion of the boat was a soporific, and it wasn't long before O'Connell wrapped himself in his coat and lay forward on a canvas-covered bundle, asleep. Brandon was no weather expert, but he had spent much of his life outdoors and habitually watched the sky. Flat, pewter-colored clouds were sliding in from the west, gradually covering the entire blue heavens. He had no idea if this indicated a change in weather was forthcoming, but there was nothing he could do about moving any faster. Already the fall of 1897 seemed to have been milder and lasted longer than he'd expected this far North.

By six that evening, they reached the foot of Lake Bennett.

"There's still plenty of daylight," Brandon said. "We're pushing on." He made the decision for all of them, hoping no one would challenge him.

"I'd sure like something to eat," Annie said quietly. "We didn't even have much breakfast."

"Sorry, Annie. Take a drink of water and cinch up your belt. We've got to make some time."

"Oh, look!" she said suddenly, pointing ahead.

"It's marked Cariboo Crossing on the map," Conrad said. "Living up to its name."

Brandon brought the boat up into the dying wind, and they drifted and watched a herd of cariboo splashing across the head of the shallow river, temporarily blocking the way to the next lake.

"What a sight!" Annie marveled at the herd of huge animals streaming across the river, ignoring the boatloads of nearby humans.

"They're heading south. Annual migration," Brandon said.

"If the animals' instincts tell them winter is coming and food will be scarce, we humans had better take warning," Conrad said.

The herd passed, and the *Cincy* headed down the river. Suddenly the boat slowed, grounded on a shallow sandbar. Brandon and Conrad removed their shoes and jumped out into the icy water to push off. Once re-floated, they dropped the sail and steered for the left bank where the swifter, deeper water ran.

Twenty minutes later they reached the head of Tagish Lake, and, with Annie pleading for them to put ashore and make camp, Brandon landed the boat near a patch of woods. The four of them went about unloading the tent and setting up camp, while they waved away swarms of mosquitoes.

After helping erect the two tents, Conrad cleaned the trout he'd caught. While Brandon brought ashore ground cover and sleeping bags, Conrad took the axe to collect some dead firewood. By the time everyone had changed into dry clothing, Conrad had the fish and a pan full of sliced potatoes sizzling over the flames.

Supper was mostly a silent meal. Everyone was tired and hungry, and the food quickly disappeared.

"Where's the bread?" George O'Connell asked.

"I didn't have time to make any," Conrad replied. "Figured we could get along without it for one meal."

O'Connell grunted and continued to stuff his mouth.

After supper, Conrad chopped more wood, and they sat as close to the smoky fire as possible to discourage the mosquitoes. The days were getting shorter, Brandon noted as the sun disappeared behind clouds across Lake Tagish. Darkness quickly settled over the patch of woods.

"Are you two going all the way to Dawson?" Conrad asked the O'Connells as he packed his pipe from a tooled leather pouch. Brandon noticed Conrad had abandoned the silver cigarette case. Either all the cigarettes were gone or wet or the silver case had disappeared in the flood at Sheep Camp.

Annie hesitated, glancing at her husband, as if waiting for him to answer.

"Yeah, we'll start out at Dawson," the lawyer finally said. He didn't elaborate. In the firelight his eyes looked puffy and irritated. Food probably soaking up some of that alcohol, Brandon thought.

Annie reached for the coffee pot.

"Ouch!" She snatched her hand from the hot handle. George only stared as Brandon wrapped a bandanna around his hand and poured her another cup. "Sorry we don't have any cream," he said.

"I saw lots of cows on the White Pass Trail," Conrad offered. "Maybe some of them will make it all the way to Dawson. I'm sure that town's short of lots of things, including milk. And it'll be a lot shorter when the river freezes and steamboats can't bring in supplies from the Outside."

Brandon silently applauded his partner for trying to get some conversation going. But George O'Connell, apparently feeling the effects of a warm fire, food,

136

fatigue, and alcohol, was dozing, his head dropping on his chest.

"I hope we brought enough food to last us," Annie said.

"Don't you worry about it, m' dear," George roused up enough to slur. "I'm here t' take care of you." He nodded off again.

Annie sipped her coffee and stared into the fire, her expression somber.

"We'll be spending some long hours on the water for the next week or so," Conrad said. "There ought to be some way we can cook on the boat so we don't have to skip meals, or land and build a fire for every meal."

"Some of the rafts and scows I saw had fires built on beds of sand," Brandon said.

Suddenly Annie's face brightened. "While I was washing up in the lake before supper, I saw a bunch of wreckage where a boat had broken up on some rocks," she said. "There was some metal half buried in the mud. Something you might be able to use to make a little stove."

"Point me in the right direction and I'll take a look before it gets too dark," Conrad said.

"About twenty yards to the right of that big tree on the bank." She pointed over her shoulder.

"Be right back." Conrad disappeared into the dusk.

Brandon looked at Annie. The gaze she returned seemed to be a silent plea for help. Her brown eyes were round and liquid, but there were dark circles under them. She was thinner than he remembered. But on the *Ohio Belle* she'd been padded by a bustle and a traveling jacket over a ruffled blouse, so it was hard to tell. He wanted to talk to her privately, but didn't know if George was asleep, or just dozing.

The lawyer's white hair shone in the firelight as he sat with his chin sunk on his chest.

Brandon took a stick and stirred the fire. Sparks flew upward into the night. He wanted to find out what had happened to her in the past few weeks, but decided to keep the conversation neutral for now. "The Mountie at Bennett told me that Tagish and its two extensions, Little Windy and Big Windy, are the roughest of any of this chain of lakes," he said.

"Why?"

"Strong and unpredictable winds." He shrugged. "Little Windy and Big Windy didn't get their names because they were mill ponds. But at least we were warned, and I'm used to handling that boat now."

Conrad came back into the firelight carrying a metal box about a foot square. "Glad you're so observant," he said to Annie, turning the box to show them the opening in one end. "It's a home-made stove that was nearly buried. I got the mud and sand rinsed out of it. There's a hole on top here for a stovepipe. It's missing, but no matter. This thing is nearly made to order. I can secure it in the bottom of the boat on a bed of sand, and we'll have a first class stove and oven. We can carry it ashore and use it in camp. I always had hired cooks at home but, with a little instruction, I'd like to try baking some bread or biscuits in this, too."

Brandon marveled that a man worth millions could be so excited over salvaging an old iron box.

138

Annie smiled, showing her white, even teeth. "I can help with the cooking, too. I'm pretty good at it." To Brandon, her interest seemed genuine. But then she lapsed into what he'd come to think of as her whipped-dog look, and she said: "I'd better get George to bed. He's worn out."

"I'll help you," Brandon offered, getting up.

"No, I can manage," she said with a wan smile. "I'm used to it," she added, as if to herself.

The partners watched as she coaxed her husband partially awake, helped him to his feet, and guided him to their tent.

After the flap dropped behind them, Conrad squatted down, rubbing remnants of mud from the oven. "I feel sorry for that woman."

"No matter what it looks like to us, they may have a perfectly happy marriage," Brandon said, smacking his neck and bringing away a hand covered with the blood of several crushed mosquitoes.

"Even as a single man, you know better than that," Conrad said in a low voice.

"Well, we can't interfere," he said. "Even if they're not happy, they might just be dependent on each other."

Conrad nodded.

Brandon changed the subject and discussed their immediate prospects for rough weather on the following day.

"If that's what's upcoming, I guess I need to roll into my sleeping bag," Conrad said, standing and stretching his slimmed-down body. "I'm healed up from the bruises and feel fine now that we're not having to pack all those heavy loads." He paused with a pensive look. "You know, when I'm busy, I'm having a lot of fun, and I wouldn't trade this for anything. And not much interrupts my sleep at night, but now and then I get to thinking about Judith and my baby son, and I sure get lonesome. I don't know what's ahead of me, but maybe, if things work out, I can bring them up here with me later on." He heaved a sigh and waved good night. "Douse that fire before you turn in. Don't want to set this dry woods ablaze."

Brandon was left sitting cross-legged on his coat, alone with his thoughts. Visions of his fiancée came to mind. He wished there were some way he could communicate with her. Was she going out with their friends? Not likely she would be sitting at home pining for his return. It seemed a long time since he'd abandoned the rut he'd fallen into. He would reserve judgment about this North country. He'd been distracted by the beauty and excitement and work, but hadn't yet reached his goal of finding some gold-bearing creek. The adventure was still unfolding. This trip might prove to be just an escape from a frustrating life, with no long-term satisfaction.

Out of the corner of his eye, he caught a movement in the shadows. His heart leaped, and he started. Then he saw it was Annie. She approached silently and knelt by the fire.

"I thought you'd gone to bed," he said.

She shook her head. "Not yet."

140

He waited for her to continue. Instead, he noticed tears glistening on her cheeks. "Want to talk about it?" he asked quietly.

She brushed her face with the back of her hand and looked at him. "I don't think I have to tell you that George is a sick man."

He nodded. "I'm really surprised he's made it this far. When I saw you sitting on that landing in Kentucky, I thought it was the last time I'd ever see you."

"He was determined that we connect with our party in Chicago, so we caught the train north."

"Why didn't you stick with them?" The painful look on her face almost made him wish he'd been more circumspect.

"You've seen how bossy and argumentative George is when he's drinking, which is most of the time. I tried to keep him under control, but two of the leaders of the party just got tired of ignoring his abrasive insults and bullying."

"You didn't bring much food or gear," he remarked.

"Most of our stuff was owned in common. When they voted us out, they just gave us what they guessed would have been our share, but it appears pretty skimpy. But with George cussing them every breath, they weren't inclined to be generous."

"Annie, this is really none of my business and you don't have to say if you don't want to, but why do you stay with him?"

She was silent for several seconds. "He's my husband," she said simply. "I took him for better or for worse. I was just a poor working girl with no prospects when we met. He literally rescued me from a dreary office job and spinsterhood. He was a charming, wealthy bachelor lawyer who was twenty years older, but had never been married. And, for some reason, he was attracted to me . . ."

"Not hard to see why," Brandon interjected.

"Thanks." She looked down. "Anyway, he was charming and swept me off my feet. I felt like the luckiest girl in the world when he proposed."

"Did he always drink this much?"

"He drank only socially when we first met. Or, at least that was all I knew about. We'd been married eight years when he became involved in a messy murder case. I don't know all the details, but he was under a lot of pressure, and I noticed him drinking more often . . . to calm his nerves, he said. I tried to help, but it was like he wanted me to be a separate part of his life . . . not a helpmate, but a plaything . . . a pretty distraction he could show off to his friends." She looked away, and her voice dropped, as if she were somehow ashamed of her perceived rôle. "He married me rather late in his life, and I think he wanted to have children, but we have not been blessed with any. Although the doctor couldn't give us the reason, I think George somehow blames me."

"Men don't generally blame themselves for that," Brandon muttered, "even if the medical fault is theirs. It might be nobody's fault."

Brandon was ill at ease counseling a stranger on marital problems, but he wanted to let her know he was there as a friend if she needed someone.

142

"Oh, and I'm so sorry about that business on the riverboat. I never got to talk to you after that."

He shook his head. "No matter. Wasn't your fault. You tried to stop him." He changed the subject. "Tell me about yourself."

The strained look on her face relaxed as she related stories of her childhood on a farm in southern Indiana. "There were eight of us kids. We had our chores and our problems, but it was mostly a happy time," she mused, a faraway look in her eyes as she sat, hugging her drawn-up knees. "I was second oldest, and, by the time I was seventeen, my parents were struggling to make a go of the farm after some crop failures and sicknesses. I left home to take some of the burden off and went to Cincinnati to look for work. I got a job in the law office of O'Connell and Gruber and went to school at night to learn typewriting since my formal education was not extensive. Not much to tell after that." She poked the coals with a stick. "George noticed me, and we began seeing each other. I wasn't attracted to him at first. But, as time went on, I saw that my prospects were limited. And George was a very sweet man. He treated me like a queen. When he proposed, I found no trouble accepting."

"Is your husband still in partnership with this Gruber?"

Her face clouded, as the reality of the present came back. "No. Mister Gruber legally dissolved the partnership when George began to drink and made some costly mistakes. They had a big row in the office one day, and George stormed out. I was still working

143

there at the time, but I quit. I think Mister Gruber gave George some kind of monetary settlement, but I don't know the details of that." She continued to stare into the dying fire. "That was four years ago. We've been doing some traveling, and I suppose we've been living on his investments and savings. Like many husbands, he's never confided in me about his finances."

"Was it just a desire for adventure that made him come north, or do you think he's actually running short of money?"

"I've wondered about that, because George has never been an outdoor person since I've known him."

They fell silent for a few seconds, while Brandon digested this possibility. He'd begun to feel sorry for George O'Connell as well as for Annie. It was amazing how one could form opinions based on first impressions.

Finally Annie yawned and stretched her arms over her head. "I suppose I need to get some sleep. If the lake is going to be as windy and rough tomorrow as you expect, I won't get any sleep on the boat. By the way" — she grinned at him — "it's been a marvelous ride! I'm loving every minute of it."

Brandon got to his feet and reached for a nearby bucket where they had earlier washed their utensils. "Walk to the lake with me while I get some water to throw on this fire."

They went into the darkness, Brandon holding her hand and finding their way through the trees by the moon on the water. He squatted to scoop up a bucketful of water by the beached boat. "If the mosquitoes weren't so bad, I think I'd sleep in the boat," he remarked.

"You could pull the hood of your sleeping bag around your face," she said. "It's getting cold out here."

"Naw. Too suffocating. It's made of heavy duck and lined with blankets," he said, straightening up. "I'll wait until it's snowing to use that sleeping bag."

She came close and put her hands on his arms. He set the bucket down. Her arms went around his neck and her cheek against his. He hugged her close for several long seconds. "Terry, thank you for listening to me," she whispered.

It was the first time in weeks he'd heard his given name. "My pleasure," he said.

"No, I mean for making me feel like I had something important to say." She kissed him on the cheek and then drew back. "As you know, George is very jealous of other men looking at me or talking to me. I just want you to know I have never been unfaithful to him, no matter what he says."

Before he could reply, she turned and disappeared into the trees toward her tent.

CHAPTER
TWELVE

Dared we that ravening terror;
heard we its din in our ears;
Called on the Gods of our fathers,
juggled forlorn with our fears;
Sank to our waists in its fury,
tossed to the sky like a fleece;
Then, when our dread was the greatest,
crashed into safety and peace.
Robert Service

The prediction of rough sailing the next day was accurate. After breakfast, they were underway by 6:30, sailing down Tagish Lake. As the morning wore on, the winds began to increase until Brandon estimated they were blowing between twenty and thirty knots.

"Coming down the long fetch of Windy Arm!" Brandon shouted at Annie and George who were huddled in the middle of the boat amidst the bales of goods. He pointed over his shoulder to the starboard side. "There's nothing to interrupt the wind. Builds up big waves."

He studied the belly of the straining sackcloth sail, trying to detect any parting seams or weak spots. The mast and stays seemed strong enough to withstand it. The white-capping waves were coming at them from the starboard quarter, rolling up under the boat,

146

carrying it along for several yards, then letting it slide back into the trough. The boat had a plunging, rolling motion that prevented Conrad from firing up his newly installed stove.

Lunch time came and went and the *Cincy* charged onward. Several times Brandon caught Annie smiling at him. While George, and even Conrad, seemed a little apprehensive at the roaring wind and waves, Annie showed no fear, even seemed to glory in it. Her smile was one of confident admiration at his skill. George seemed not to notice, as he nipped at an apparently bottomless pocket flask.

When Brandon finally grew tired of his constant vigilance, steering and handling the mainsheet, he signaled for Conrad to come relieve him. His partner climbed carefully back to the stern, and Brandon gave him some quick instructions and then sat with him for several minutes while he got the feel of it. "Doesn't handle much like my ketch at home, but the theory's the same!" Conrad shouted in Brandon's ear. He grinned and corrected their course as a wave attempted to slew the stern around.

Twenty minutes later, in a moment of inattention, Conrad allowed the *Cincy* to get broadside to the four-foot waves. The heavy wind was pressing them down at the same time and water poured over the side. Brandon sprang to the mast, jerked the halyard loose, and dropped the sail. The laden boat staggered drunkenly, rolling from side to side as it straightened up. Annie was frantically bailing with a bucket.

147

They were wet and chilled when Brandon nosed the boat into the bank among several dozen boats, canoes, and scows at three that afternoon.

"Why are we stopping here?" Annie asked.

"This is Tagish House . . . police headquarters," Brandon replied, stretching his stiff leg muscles. "The Mounties have to inspect all passing boats."

She looked another question at him.

"They want to be sure everyone has adequate food and gear," he explained. "They'll also search for liquors and tobacco, to collect extra duty. Anything beyond a personal amount of alcohol will be confiscated, I'm told, unless you have a saloonkeeper's permit."

A look of alarm crossed her face. "George can't have his liquor confiscated," she whispered, glancing apprehensively around. "I can't handle him if he's suddenly deprived of his drink."

"How much has he got?"

"Six cases of his favorite brandy and whisky."

"Wait here." Brandon went to strike up a conversation with several men in a nearby line.

He returned several minutes later. "Word is, we can probably bribe the inspecting officer," he reported to the three of them. "Several men in that line gave the officer a dollar each to issue their inspection slips without ever going near their boats. Not so much contraband. They just didn't want to wait."

"What's that long line for?" Conrad asked.

"Have to turn in the inspection slip at police headquarters . . . the long house yonder. Someone there issues our clearance papers."

148

"More damned falderol," George mumbled, staying in the background.

A few minutes later, Brandon found the inspecting officer near the beach, working his way through the cluster of roughly dressed men around him. "Officer, we're in an awful big hurry," he said, slipping the red-coated policeman a crisp, folded dollar bill. The Mountie took the money without comment and thrust it into his pocket. "What's your boat number?"

"Nineteen fifty-two."

The policeman scribbled something in a small notebook, tore the page out, and handed it to Brandon. "Next!"

Brandon held up the slip of paper to the others as he went to the end of a long line that wound its slow way to the Tagish House. "Go get some dry clothes and find something to eat," he told them. "Looks like I'll be here a while."

He held his position, shifting from one leg to another, and even sitting on the ground until evening when everyone was given a number for his place in line. He was handed number 281, written on a gum wrapper, apparently the most convenient material at hand.

They all slept rather restlessly in the boat, tucked in among the sacks and bales. The next day Brandon stood wearily in line until one in the afternoon when he finally reached headquarters and secured the necessary clearance papers. They shoved off at 1:30.

The wind was still strong and the lake rough, but they made good time before twilight found them aground in the shallow river connecting Tagish Lake and Marsh Lake. They were able to push free with the sweeps, then were forced to shove off a second grounding a few minutes later. They sailed another nineteen miles and set up camp in the dark at the lower end of Marsh Lake.

The next day they got a reprieve when they entered Fifty-Mile River which had a moderate current. Here they were able to rest and enjoy a smoke while they drifted along, paying only minimal attention to steering. Conrad again caught a trout and grilled it on his stove for lunch. Beans and hard crackers completed the fare.

George O'Connell talked only in spurts. At times he was silent for hours at a stretch; at others, he blustered and grumbled, casting baleful looks at Brandon and Conrad. Brandon thought he'd probably never take another drink himself, if alcohol made him as unhappy as this man seemed to be. O'Connell gave the impression of being in his own world, disconnected from reality. Maybe continued heavy drinking had damaged his brain. In any case, Brandon knew the former attorney was capable of violence and kept a wary eye on him.

The low banks of the river were lined with dark green spruce, the predominant species here. Only a few golden leaves still clung to the aspens.

Brandon had killed time in line at Tagish House talking to several men near him, men who were familiar with this stretch of water. They had confirmed what he'd heard before. "Pull ashore before you reach Miles

150

Cañon," they had told him. "Walk along the high bank and watch other boats. Pick the right line to go through, or there's a good chance you'll capsize or smash up."

A bearded man nearby had nodded. "Sure enough. I lost a good friend there two weeks ago. You're lucky if you just lose your outfit and not your life. Even if you don't drown, that cold water will do for ya. Bodies don't even come to the surface in that icy water."

"I been through there twice," the first man had said. "Crazy, I guess, but I'm coming back for a third try. Found out I was pretty good at it, and got hired by another party to take 'em through. Good pay. I guess the gold can wait a little longer for me."

Brandon had taken a closer look at the fearless little man. He was unshaven and weather-beaten, but sinewy under his dirty canvas clothing. Brandon judged him younger than he first appeared.

But these warnings were only a vague memory in Brandon's mind as the *Cincy* drifted on the peaceful river. A good meal, a pipe, and a rare absence of wind combined to lull him into a sense of safety and well-being.

As a result, Brandon hardly noticed the cluster of boats moored to the bank as they drifted past. He saw the banks of the river drawing closer and moving along faster on either side. The river was being squeezed, and its current picking up speed. A distant roar set off an alarm bell in his head. The import of the moored boats suddenly registered on his consciousness. He dropped his pipe into the bilge water at his feet and scrambled for the tiller.

"Conrad, get on those oars! Pull for the bank!"

Brandon yanked the rudder loose and fitted one of two long steering sweeps in its place. A minute of hard rowing brought them several yards closer to the left bank.

"Give us a hand!" Brandon yelled to a man ashore who was wading out to help. "Annie, take that rope in the bow and throw it to that man on shore!" he cried. "Quick!"

Without a word, the woman crawled forward over the piled cargo and snatched up the coiled rope. Pivoting her body, she flung it. The wet line snaked through the air, uncoiling as it went, and fell across the shoulder of the man ashore who'd seen their plight and was standing knee-deep, ready to grab the stem post when the boat got close. He gripped the rope, wrapping it around both hands and one arm, then threw himself back on his heels as the boat shot past.

It was no contest. The man was jerked forward, tumbling over one of the moored boats, and landed headfirst in the water before he could let go of the line.

They were in the grip of the current now. With no steerageway, the boat was spun around, stern-first, as the river rushed toward the narrow cañon. The boat was carried around a bend, and the banks on either side grew steeper. An icy fist clutched Brandon's stomach as he looked over his shoulder. A louder roar of tumbling water echoed off the vertical walls of Miles Cañon.

"Pull on one oar!" he shouted. "Bring her head around!" He leaned on the steering oar to aid Conrad's efforts.

They spun the craft around, with her bow again pointing downstream. Another bend cut off all views ahead. The river widened out slightly. Then, just ahead, the smooth, slick current was sucking into the narrow cleft. Brandon's stomach contracted. The roar grew deafening and blunted his shout to Conrad to aim for the center of the passage. The boat was accelerated into the cañon. Jagged, vertical walls of basalt rose up a hundred feet on either side of them. Brandon sat in the stern, bracing his feet and steering the boat as near to the middle of the river as he could. The bow dropped suddenly into a hole, then leaped skyward, throwing spray. Down it plunged again, white water roaring and foaming all around them.

As if some giant had grabbed them, the boat lurched sideways, out of control. Brandon threw all his weight against the steering sweep. The oar snapped off in his hands, sending him sprawling, banging both arms against the gunwale. He struggled up, catching a fleeting glimpse of several anxious faces watching from the top of the cliff. Ignoring the pain in his arms, he grabbed the spare sweep as the boat was spun in a half circle. Black boulders shot past barely five feet away. Bracing with his knees, he finally got the steering oar in place, just as the boat was swept out into a wider spot in the river.

He and Conrad managed to turn the bow downstream.

"That way!" Brandon shouted, making an instantaneous decision and shoving the oar to starboard. The swifter water was being flung against the left side of the cañon, forming a ridge of smoother water along the rock wall. Riding this ridge was a perilous move. If they clipped the jagged cliff face, the boat would be flung sideways into the foaming torrent and capsize, losing boat, supplies, and their lives. But this was not a reasoned decision; it was an instinctive gamble. And it worked. The vertical rock whizzed past them in a black blur. Seconds were eternity as Brandon held his breath and balanced the open boat along the higher ridge of rushing water like a two-ton projectile.

Out of the corner of his eye, Brandon saw the second narrow cut whip past, then they plunged down a six-foot drop. Leaping, frothing, mad water churned around and over them, the boat pitching and yawing.

Suddenly the *Cincy* shot out below the cañon into a wider river, and the boat spun lazily into quieter water.

Brandon saw a half dozen boats pulled up on the right-hand bank. The current was still swift; less than a mile ahead were the fearful White Horse Rapids.

"Pull for the shore!" Brandon yelled.

Conrad complied.

They were being carried down toward a raft stranded on some rocks just ahead, and Brandon cursed under his breath as the sweep barely altered the heading of the laden *Cincy*. Just as he was bracing himself for the crash, the bow swung right a few degrees, and they were carried past the wrecked raft. But they were still

154

nearly powerless in the grip of the river and could only gradually angle across the current.

As they finally approached the bank, the boat scraped over a submerged rock, then crunched another with a sickening sound. They came to stop, firmly grounded, twenty feet from shore. A man threw them a line, and Conrad made it fast to the bow. Thus secured by several willing hands ashore holding the rope, Brandon and Conrad pulled on their rubber boots and stepped out into the shallow, swift water. For several minutes they struggled to push the boat free, but with no luck. Slipping on the moss-covered rocks, Brandon's feet shot out from under him, and he grabbed the edge of the boat to keep the current from carrying him away.

Finally the two men helped Annie and George O'Connell over the side, and the four of them waded ashore. O'Connell, apparently drunker than usual, muttered something, yet didn't even gripe or curse at wetting his legs in the icy water.

Over the next three hours, with the help of three strangers, they hauled their entire outfit ashore. Once the boat was refloated and pulled ashore, Brandon discovered a substantial leak where one of its bottom planks had been splintered next to the keel. They spent the rest of the day collecting and stuffing the crack with moss, then sealing it with sap collected from the coniferous trees. It was a makeshift repair at best, but they'd gotten used to bilge water from slow leaks, waves, and spray coming over the side.

"We've been damned lucky so far," Conrad remarked later that day, as he tried to rub the sticky sap from his hands. "I don't mind telling you there were a couple of times, I thought we would capsize back there. Pretty scary." His wet, black hair was plastered down to his skull, his face drawn and pale. "You think it might be a good idea to hire a pilot to take us through White Horse Rapids? These men who helped us here say they know a pilot who charges twenty-five dollars."

Brandon considered this for several seconds as he stared out at the relentless river rushing past them. "That's a lot of money just to get downriver another couple of miles."

"Might keep us from losing our whole outfit, though," Conrad said.

"I doubt anyone we could hire here has much more than three or four trips to count as his whole experience."

Conrad shrugged. "Just a thought."

"I think we can do it by ourselves. You've been good on the oars."

Conrad didn't reply.

"And the O'Connells haven't been any problem."

They both stared off in the distance where Annie and George were struggling to erect their tent about fifty yards away on a level spot of ground.

"I think Annie was scared spitless and the old man was too drunk to care," Conrad said. "But I'll defer to your judgment. If you think we can make it OK, I'm game. Right now, I'm dog tired and wet and cold and think I'll get Annie to steal me a bottle of her husband's brandy to warm up with."

"I couldn't handle any of that stuff right now." Brandon grinned. "I'll get us a campfire going, if you want to break out some grub." He didn't want to admit how tired he was. For some reason he couldn't explain, he had assumed a leadership rôle, possibly because of his boating skills, even though his previous experience had been confined to sailing on the Ohio River. Maybe Conrad was not a natural leader of men, and his retiring personality had balked at assuming the top job in a family company that would force this kind of leadership on him.

Early next morning, a thin layer of ice fringed the quiet water at the river's edge, and Brandon could see his breath as he stooped to fill their coffee pot. But the sun quickly dissipated the chill as they worked to load the boat once more.

With George and Annie lending their weight to effort, the four dragged the boat upstream about a hundred feet above the worst of the flat rocks, then climbed in and shoved off. For the next hour, Brandon guided them down the middle of the river. The boat leaped and plunged, throwing a chilling spray over them as they huddled down in their jackets. The water was low, and the shoreline of the river on both sides was wide and rocky.

Brandon was alert this time and ran the boat ashore as soon as he could make out the beginnings of White Horse Rapids in the distance.

"Time to lighten ship," he announced. He and Conrad climbed out and began unloading.

"I ain't unloading a damn' thing!" George announced, keeping his seat on a thwart.

"Just ignore him for now," Annie whispered as she pitched in to help.

Twenty minutes later, Conrad straightened up, panting. "That enough? Looks like about twelve-hundred pounds."

"Yeah. She's riding high enough now," Brandon said. "Let's go."

They pushed off and turned the boat into the cañon where the current sucked them along faster, and ever faster. The express-train speed was almost dizzying, and Brandon tried to keep his eyes focused directly ahead and away from the shoreline unreeling on both sides of them. But the boat was more buoyant now and handled easier. Without most of its ballast, it was thrown up and plunged down in the rolling water. Brandon held his breath and pointed the bow straight ahead. With a mighty surging roar, white water foamed over and around huge boulders as they lanced through the narrow White Horse. They shot over a six-foot fall and dropped. The flat bottom of the hull smacked the surface below, and the boat shuddered from end to end. As if shaking itself free of the swift water, the *Cincy* slowed and drifted into a wider channel.

Brandon heaved a great sigh and brought the boat ashore about a quarter mile below the rapids.

With George O'Connell sleeping in the boat, the three of them spent the rest of the morning and early afternoon packing the twelve-hundred pounds of goods down and reloading them into the boat.

158

"What's the matter? Lose something?" Brandon asked as they stopped to rest after their fourth trip and he noticed Annie frowning at their pile of supplies.

"George had four cases of brandy and two of Kentucky bourbon," she said. "I haven't seen them anywhere."

"They're probably in the boat. I doubt he'd let them out of his sight," Brandon said.

She shook her head. "No. I specifically remember unloading them."

They made a thorough search of the boat, then returned upstream for a last load.

"It's missing!" she cried, almost desperately. "Somebody stole it while we were shooting the rapids."

Brandon and Conrad looked at each other. How would a suddenly sober O'Connell react to being deprived of his alcoholic sedative?

"Maybe it will be the saving of him," Conrad finally said. "He couldn't continue to drink like that for very long without killing himself."

Annie was almost tearful. "You don't know how mean he can be when he sobers up. Terry remembers what he was like on the riverboat."

It was a prospect Brandon didn't want to contemplate.

CHAPTER
THIRTEEN

**Fine specimens of manhood
they would reckon us out there;
It's the tracking and the packing
and the poling in the sun;
It's the sleeping in the open,
it's the rugged, unfaked food;
It's the snowshoe and the paddle,
and the campfire and the gun . . .**
Robert Service

It was five in the afternoon before they resumed their trip down the Fifty-Mile River. All but George O'Connell were fatigued from the strain of running the White Horse Rapids and packing their goods. They raised the square sail, but the whisper of breeze hardly stirred it, so this day they just let the current do the work.

Brandon caught himself dozing at the tiller. The air was chill, but he had his jacket on with the collar turned up and his felt hat pulled down. With no wind, the autumn sun felt good. A torpor fell over the little party, George O'Connell dozing with the rest. Brandon attributed this to the fact that he still had some brandy or whisky in his silver pocket flask and had not yet discovered the loss of his stash of alcohol. Any one of several hundred passersby could have stolen it,

Brandon thought. If he had known it was there, he'd either have not unloaded it, or he would have taken greater pains to hide it from any curious eyes. All kinds of goods had been abandoned along the trail, and nobody looked at them a second time. But good quality beverage alcohol had universal value that nearly rivaled gold, except that it was more perishable. It could be sold for cash or traded for any number of things, with white men or Indians.

The river, they discovered, was very low, and full of silt and sandbars. They ran aground twice, but pushed off with the oars without getting out of the boat. By dark they'd landed to camp near the head of Lake Laberge.

After an early breakfast, they set out again, rowing at first to get clear of the sandbars. Then Conrad hoisted the sail, and they had a fair wind until nearly noon. Then a perfect calm fell over the lake, and they resumed rowing for an hour before they landed on a large island to stretch their legs and eat some lunch. Conrad's trolling had produced no fish, so they dug out some bacon to fry with the remains of several potatoes they salvaged from black rot.

"Beautiful mountains around here," Annie remarked after lunch, strolling to the water's edge to take a look around.

Brandon was puffing his pipe to life, then ground the match under his foot. "I prefer forested mountains," he said, "rather than these bald knobs."

161

They stood silently, sucking in the bracing air and the view. Pans were clattering in the background as Conrad cleaned up, a job he'd volunteered for. "If you can handle the boat, the least I can do is try to cook and wash up."

"I don't think I could've made a better choice for a partner if I'd had a thousand applicants for the job, and a year to interview them," Brandon remarked to Annie, jerking his head toward Conrad.

"Wish I could say the same," she replied wistfully, as George O'Connell went down the slope a few yards away with the undue care of the inebriated, and stepped into the boat. "Bacchus has replaced me as his first love."

They watched the lawyer rummage around in the piles of supplies. After a minute or two, he raised up and looked around belligerently. Then he resumed his digging.

"You know what he's looking for," she said quietly.

Brandon took his pipe from his mouth and spat. "Yeah. I'd hoped he had enough on him to last another day or so."

She sighed. "Might as well brace myself for the fireworks. As soon as he starts to really sober up and feel bad, I'm the first one he'll accuse of taking his bottles."

"And I'll be the second," Brandon said. "Is he armed?"

"I hid his ammunition, but couldn't get the loaded Derringer he always carries. He even sleeps with it on a heavy cord around his neck."

"I'm not going to let him get by with abusing you," Brandon said.

162

"I appreciate it, but I can probably handle him. At least let me try. Don't interfere unless you have to." She looked sideways at him. "Promise?"

"OK." He knocked the dottle out of his pipe on the heel of his boot. "We'd better get started."

The calm continued, and Brandon and Conrad alternated at the oars for the rest of the day.

The next day a strong headwind was blowing, so they rowed into a chop for ten grueling miles and finally stopped to camp at the foot of Lake Laberge.

"Time for you to spell us at the oars," Brandon told George O'Connell the next morning. "It's not far to Thirty-Mile River, so it won't be too bad."

Like the other two men, George had not bathed or shaved in days. Unlike the other two, he was looking bleary-eyed and emaciated. Gray stubble glistened on his sagging cheeks in the wan sunshine that strove to penetrate the icy morning fog. The lawyer's woolen jacket hung limply from his shoulders. He'd been subsisting on brandy and little else. This morning, after several bites of bacon and flapjacks and a drink of coffee, he had promptly vomited up everything.

He drew himself up and looked at them haughtily. "You forget, I paid for this gaw-damn' boat. I'm the owner *and* the captain. And the captain does not row. Now, get on with it before I fire you all."

Brandon had to turn away to hide a grin. The man was pitiful and had no intention of being funny, but, as Brandon turned toward the boat, he quickly forgot about the old man. The heavy fog was dissipating, and sunlight glinted strangely off the flat water of the lake.

163

But it wasn't water at all. Glare ice coated the surface for fifty yards out from shore. The freeze-up had come overnight while he had slept warm in his bedroll. His heart leaped. Were they iced in on the shores of Lake Laberge?

He climbed into the boat, took an oar, and began jabbing at the ice alongside. To his relief the coating was only about an inch thick and broke easily.

"Let's get moving."

They needed no urging. Conrad untied the bow from a tree and shoved off. Then he took up an oar in the bow and punched the ice, breaking it into large sheets that tilted up and slid away from them as Brandon sculled the boat along with side-to-side thrusts of the steering sweep.

The ice had not formed in the middle of the lake, and Conrad took his place on a thwart to row. A half hour of steady rowing brought them to Thirty-Mile River, a fast-flowing stretch of water.

"According to the map, this is the head of the Lewis River," Brandon said, steering with one hand and holding the folded map on his knee with the other. He tucked the map inside his jacket and pulled down his hat to shield his eyes from the sun's glare as they entered the swift water. "No danger of this freezing up for a while," he called to Conrad. "Get up front and keep look-out for shoals and rocks."

He had hardly finished talking when the boat struck a rock, then bumped four or five more times before coming to a stop.

164

The *Cincy* was grounded fast on the flat rocks in the middle of the narrow river. Several boats darted past to the left, but the men in them had no chance to help, since they had their own hands full.

Brandon held his breath, but the stern did not come around. "I don't dare let go of the steering sweep. If we swing around broadside and don't come off this rock, the current is strong enough to swamp us."

"I'll get us off," Conrad said, pulling on his rubber boots and climbing over the side. He slipped and slid and strained for ten minutes, and finally managed to set the boat adrift.

"A flat-bottom boat is just what we need in this shallow water with all these rocks and sandbars," Brandon said as the vegetation unreeled past them at a twelve-mile-an-hour clip. "That six-inch keel probably kept us from bashing a hole in the bottom back there."

"And if it hadn't been for that keel, we probably would have cleared that rock completely," Conrad shot back with a grin.

"Oh, my God!" George O'Connell screamed. "Get 'em out! Get 'em out of the boat!"

"What?"

"Snakes! They're crawling up my legs. Help! Somebody get 'em off me!"

Chills ran up Brandon's spine as he let go of the steering sweep and lunged forward over the piles of supplies. Annie and Conrad were already there.

"Get 'em off!" George clawed at his legs, his eyes wild and frantic.

"No snakes," Conrad said, shaking his head.

"George! George! Calm down," Annie said, shaking his shoulders and looking into his face. "There aren't any snakes. It's all right."

"Yes! Yes! Right there! Don't you see them?" George screamed.

Brandon locked his arms around the older man and pulled him down onto some sacks in the bottom of the boat. "Get some rope," he breathed to Conrad. "He's having the d.t.'s. We'll have to restrain him until he calms down."

"You can't tie him up in his condition!" Annie cried, biting her lip.

"He's liable to jump overboard if we don't," Conrad said. "A reaction to his liquor being cut off suddenly."

George was still wailing and crying piteously to be rescued from the imaginary reptiles.

"Talk to him, Annie," Brandon said, holding George down, while Conrad produced the extra rope. "See if you can break through. Let him know you're there and that he's safe."

The boat was drifting out of control for several minutes while they got George restrained. Luckily Brandon got back to the steering oar just in time to prevent the boat from going aground on a sandbar.

The next two hours were a constant challenge to Brandon who had to spot and dodge gravel bars and rocks. They were moving so fast, and the river had so many bends, there was no time to relax.

Coming around a sharp bend, he saw a red-lettered sign stuck up on the left shore some distance away.

"Is that some kind of warning?"

166

Conrad twisted around from his seat at the oars. "Can't read it from here."

Their eyes were riveted on the sign for the next several seconds.

"It says . . . 'Danger . . . Keep to the Right'!" Conrad yelled, pointing.

Brandon saw the rocks directly in their way, and the wreck of a boat sticking up out of the water.

"Pull for your life!" he yelled at Conrad.

His yell was unnecessary. The wiry Conrad tugged at the oars, even rising up out of his seat with the effort to angle the heavy boat across the swift current.

Brandon was sculling with the steering oar, then finally pushed it away from him as far as he could in an attempt to go to starboard. The *Cincy* sluggishly responded, but was being carried downstream so fast he couldn't judge the rapidly closing distance. The wreckage rushed up to meet them. Brandon held his breath, bracing himself. Conrad's oar blade caught the rock, whipping the handle back across his chest. He tumbled backward as the boat was thrown sideways, spinning away past the boulder.

Brandon quickly got the boat under control before it rammed the right-hand bank. As soon as it was headed downstream again, he jumped forward. "You hurt?"

Annie was helping Conrad to a sitting position as he held his chest. "No. Just knocked the wind out of me," he gasped. "It caught me flat across the chest. Probably have a good bruise there tomorrow."

Brandon scrambled back to the steering sweep as the boat began to yaw out of control. Some hundred yards below them a boat had been swamped. Even from this distance, he could see sacks and boxes floating free, and heads bobbing in the water. Another party on the left bank was going to their rescue. Most of their food either sunk or ruined by the water, Brandon thought, with a pang of compassion for the unfortunate strangers.

Ten minutes later, Brandon's heart jumped into his throat as the six-inch keel of their speeding boat grated across a flat rock and kept going. The rocks were visible under the clear water, but the refraction made it impossible to tell how deep they were. Brandon just had to steer and hope. If he guessed wrong, their weight and speed would bash the bottom out of the boat. Thirty-Mile River was the worst he'd seen so far. He would have much preferred the boiling rapids. At least they were over quickly. But he would not have any of his passengers know his fear. He set his face grimly and concentrated as the hours dragged by.

Before they camped that night, George O'Connell's hallucinations had passed, but he was sick and retired to his tent early without eating supper.

"First time he's been sober in weeks," Annie confided to them at their campfire. "But he's a very sick man."

"I think you need to find a doctor for him when you get to Dawson," Brandon said. "Not that he could probably do much for him, unless he has other problems I don't know about."

She simply nodded, looking down at her plate. Brandon noticed a tear sliding down her cheek, and was suddenly very sorry for her. "Why don't you take some of that fresh fish in to him and see if he'll eat."

"I will." She reached to spoon up another helping of beans. The firelight glinted from a gold pin on her jacket.

"Annie, I've been meaning to ask you about that gold pin you always wear on the outside," Brandon said.

"Oh, it's a little pin with my initials my mother gave me when I turned thirteen. It belonged to her mother whom I was named for."

Brandon leaned closer to look at the ornate script of the gold ornament. "These letters are AMH."

"My grandmother's name was Anna Marie Hosher."

"Beautiful."

"It's one of the few things I still have to remember my family."

The days were growing rapidly shorter, and they retired just after supper. Next morning they arose before daylight and ate a hurried breakfast of warmed-over flapjacks and coffee. George O'Connell looked like a walking corpse in the gray light of early morning as they shoved the boat into the stream and started once again. His hands shook with a palsy that made him appear very aged.

"Seems like we've been on these streams and lakes forever," Brandon remarked, settling at the steering oar which he used constantly now in favor of the smaller rudder and tiller. He said nothing to Annie and Conrad, but the leaden sky and the heavy, hard cold

169

was ominous. By mid-morning, a few feathery snowflakes began to drift silently down. No one said anything. Brandon switched hands on the steering oar, putting one in his pocket to keep his fingers from getting numb. What day of the month was it? They'd been on the water for about two weeks, as nearly as he could remember. Second or third week of October was his closest guess. He had set his watch to local time at Chilkoot, and had remembered to wind it each day since, but time in this country was measured now by the dwindling number of daylight hours. His ears and toes were getting cold; his breath was steam in the still air. Looking around, he saw two other boats in the distance, one ahead of them and one behind. The procession was still ongoing, even in the teeth of a closing winter. Some of them would make it to Dawson; others would not.

Shortly before noon they reached Hootalinqua where the Teslin River flowed into the Lewis from the southeast. They pulled ashore near several other boats while another group of red-coated Canadian police inspected their papers.

"You're past the toughest part," a corporal replied to Conrad's question. "The river widens from here down. Five-Finger Rapids are about the only dangerous water you have ahead of you now."

By two o'clock they were on their way again. The country-side had flattened out around them, with mountains visible in the distance. By five o'clock they were forced to camp in the fast-fading light.

170

As soon as dawn allowed them to see, they were again drifting on the slower current of the Lewis River. "We have a fifty-mile run along here," Brandon told Annie as she spooned hot, thick soup into her husband's mouth as he lay bundled up in wool blankets against the wet chill. During the past two days, he had survived the agony of a hangover and the sickness of withdrawal from alcoholic poisoning. Annie had taken on the job of bringing him back from malnourishment. So far he'd been too sick and weak to accuse anyone of taking his liquor. With the boat stable, Conrad was able to build a fire in his tiny stove and heat some tinned soup from their stores. He had even taken to mixing up some biscuit dough to practice his new-found interest in baking.

Unlike Thirty-Mile River, the Lewis was murky and full of glacial silt. Brandon could hear a continuous hissing sound as the silt slid past the sides and bottom of the boat. The Lewis also flowed around numerous islands and gravel bars. By eight-thirty, they reached the confluence of the Big Salmon River and another log post staffed by Mounties that they'd been told to watch for. They were not required to stop, but saw a policeman ashore with field glasses and a pad of paper recording the registration numbers of all vessels that passed.

The mouth of the Little Salmon River was passed by four o'clock.

"I hear tell gold was discovered along both the Big Salmon and the Little Salmon Rivers," Brandon remarked as they floated past. "But I don't see a sign of any claims being worked."

"Could be farther upstream out of sight," Conrad said. "Then again, when rumors are repeated often enough, they take on the substance of fact. I've seen it happen in the business world more than once."

They pulled in and made camp just before dark. Without being asked, Annie took the small axe and went after firewood. Pieces of dry driftwood and dead windfalls were everywhere. Even though they'd selected a partially protected site in a copse of evergreens, the wind began to pick up and Brandon had trouble getting the fire started inside the rock ring he constructed. By the time supper was cooked and they were squatting and sitting around eating, the wind was roaring overhead in the treetops with a mournful wailing noise.

"The sound of that wind makes it feel even colder," Conrad said to no one in particular, turning up his coat collar as a gust swirled up sparks from the fire.

Brandon was trying to calculate how much farther it was to Dawson. Except for the problem of shelter, he was beginning to think he would like to avoid the several thousand Cheechakos who were descending on Dawson. He wondered if they might be better off stopping near the Stewart River, about seventy-two miles this side of the town. It might already be too late to do much prospecting.

"Starting in the morning, we have to make a dash for it," Brandon announced after they'd finished eating. Curious looks came from the other three, including George who seemed more alert. "That means we start and just keep going every minute that we have enough daylight. No stopping to eat, or for anything else, except total darkness. Conrad, you and I will take turns steering, rowing, or handling sail. Annie can spell us . . . and George, too, if you feel up to it."

The lawyer merely stared at him with no expression.

"We'll cook what food we can on the boat. If we get a clear night, with moonlight, we'll keep going and take turns sleeping. If we don't hurry, we'll never make Dawson before freeze-up, which could come at any time. Maybe this wind and the swift current in that river out there will keep the ice from forming tonight, at least. We need to push as hard as we can." He looked around at the anxious faces in the firelight. "Agreed?"

"Fine by me," Conrad said.

"The sooner we get there, the better," Annie murmured.

Even George O'Connell, who seemed to have come back to join them, nodded his acquiescence.

CHAPTER
FOURTEEN

There's a land where the mountains are nameless,
And the rivers all run God knows where;
There are lives that are erring and aimless,
And deaths that just hang by a hair . . .
Robert Service

The blowing snowflakes were so thick Brandon could only dimly make out Five-Finger Rapids dead ahead. A policeman at the Mountie post where they'd last stopped told him this final major obstacle was composed of five large and small rocky islands that jutted up across the width of the river's channel. "The only safe way to get by is through the right-hand chute. There's probably thirty yards between a rocky island on your left and a steep cliff on the mainland to your right. The water's a little rough, especially if the wind's blowing counter to the current, but you've already survived a lot rougher water getting this far."

The Mountie's reassuring words echoed in Brandon's head as he slitted his eyes against the feathery flakes that were melting on his face and eyelashes. He lined up the boat on the right-hand passage. The wind was funneling through this slot directly into their faces, and he was thankful they didn't have to try to rely on the awkward square sail that was now being used as an

174

additional cover for the goods and passengers. The strong current would take them through. He flexed his mittened fingers on the steering sweep, and looked down at the three inches of bilge water that continually sloshed back and forth under the floorboards that lay, unattached, across the ribs in the bottom. If there was one thing they had to be cautious of from here on, it was keeping themselves dry. Bitter cold had not yet set in, but wet feet, head, or hands could lead to a quick loss of body heat, sickness, and possibly death if one of them should happen to fall into the water.

The *Cincy* picked up speed, and the granite walls of the channel loomed up blacker out of the swirling snow. A few black spruce trees spiked the gray sky. Conrad, stationed in the bow, motioned with his arm and pointed at the middle of the chute. The boat dipped and plowed into a wave. A sheet of spray was thrown into the air and spattered down on the canvas sack sail that covered the supplies.

Brandon braced his feet as the boat began to pitch and roll. He squinted into the sleet that was now stinging his face. He'd neglected to buy a winter hat, but had substituted a woolen scarf tied over his head and under his chin to keep his ears warm. He wore his broad-brimmed hat atop this, secured against the wind by a leather thong he'd fashioned into a chin strap.

After only a few minutes of rough water, they were once more in the clear and were drifting in a world of white as the islands of Five-Finger Rapids disappeared rapidly behind them.

"I think we're home free," Conrad said. "Let's celebrate." He shoved some small hunks of dry driftwood into his stove. "I'll whip up some hot stew."

"Milton, you're a wonder," Annie said from under the blanket pulled over her head and shoulders. "How do you keep up such good spirits in this miserable, wet weather?"

They spent the night in the boat, tied up to a bank, but went ashore to build a campfire and eat a good breakfast just before dawn. The snow had stopped. But the real cold was now beginning to grip the land. The sun rose lower in a bitter blue sky, shedding light, but no warmth.

They set off just as it was light enough to see, and in the late afternoon they passed Fort Selkirk, situated on the high left-hand bank of the river.

"Doesn't look like much, does it?" Conrad said, indicating the several log huts they could barely see from their low station in the boat.

"Those are probably the huts where the Indians live," Brandon said. "There's a Mounted Police detachment here. Wish I knew something about the history of this old fort."

"Well, we're now officially on the Yukon River," Conrad said to Annie. "It looks like the same river on the map, but the Lewis changes its name to the Yukon River from here down."

Brandon saw four other boats as dark specks far out over the water, two with sails up, trying to get downstream a little faster than the current could carry them. Other rivers and creeks fed into the Yukon, swelling it to a width of about three-quarters of a mile at this point. They had their own sail up, and it aided their speed with a very light breeze. But the thing he didn't mention that concerned him most was the mush ice drifting into the river from the shallower streams.

By the time a short dusk was stealing over the river, he'd decided to push on into the clear night. The need for speed was urgent, and the width and steady current of the river would keep them relatively safe. The others were agreeable, when Brandon pointed out the ever-increasing drifting ice.

"Spell me about midnight," he said to Conrad after the other three finished eating and were squirming down among the sacks and boxes to find a relatively comfortable bed for the night.

The next morning they were all stiff and cold and took turns stretching and bending in the boat to stimulate some circulation. Hot coffee with sugar helped the process.

Brandon was distracted, watching the increasing ice flow in the murky water. Anchor ice was rising from the bottom of the river, adding to the mush ice drifting in from tributaries. When the boat rode closer to the bank, he could see rim ice stretching its long fingers out over the quieter water near the shore. The liquid in the giant arteries of the North was congealing.

It was a race against time and nature now, and the four Argonauts huddled in the boat the rest of that day and night, miserably cold, encouraging one another, sometimes with a wry joke. Eating and napping, they somehow drifted through the long night. Whenever necessary, they held up a blanket to give one another privacy when using the bailing bucket for a slop jar.

Early next morning, an hour after daylight, they came to the confluence of the Stewart River. By mutual consent, they landed on the smaller of two islands near the mouth of the Stewart.

They climbed out, stiff with cold, inactivity, and fatigue, and walked up through the spruce trees. Fifty yards in they came to an old, abandoned, one-room log cabin with two gaping windows and a plank door that was still sturdy. A rusty stovepipe poked up through the roof at an angle.

Brandon looked in one of the glassless windows. He could make out nothing but a table and a stone fireplace in the dim interior. Sniffing the musty odor of long disuse, he said: "Cold, but livable." He turned to Conrad. "I think we ought to stop right here. Rumor has it that good color has been found along the Stewart and nearby creeks."

A look of alarm crossed Annie's face. "What about us?"

"We ain't holing up in no gaw-damned shack in the middle of the river!" George O'Connell grated, a sour look on his face.

"Dawson is about seventy-five miles farther downriver," Brandon continued. "If that's where you want to go, you'd best get going right away. It's your boat. You can keep it, sell it, or burn it for firewood when you get there."

"You really expect us to go on by ourselves?" Annie asked.

"That's what your husband wants. You can handle the boat with no trouble. Don't even have to use the sail. The current will take you there. Buck up, Annie," he said, sensing her tension. "You can do it. Have confidence in yourself."

They were walking back toward the boat. As George lagged behind, Brandon moved closer to her and said quietly: "You can't stay here. George would go mad without his liquor. He didn't make this trip to do any hard prospecting. I don't know what your plans are, but you'd be better off in town. After you get there, you and George can decide what to do next."

She gave him an anguished look.

"It's the best thing, Annie. He needs to be around people, and he probably needs a doctor. Besides, there's liquor there, and he has money in his pocket. But you won't be isolated. And there will be other women."

His words seemed to have little comforting effect as they reached the boat and began unloading their supplies. Before they finished, Conrad had hailed a passing boat with two men in it. They pulled in, thinking the beached party needed help. They turned out to be a German and an Irishman from St. Louis and said they'd be more than glad to escort the couple the last seventy-five miles to Dawson.

Brandon wanted to say more reassuring words to Annie before they parted, maybe give her a hug, but had no opportunity as the two St. Louis men were eager to be off.

"Good luck, George," Conrad said, shaking the lawyer's hand as if they'd been the best of friends. "Thanks for sharing your boat with us. We'll probably be in town in a few weeks looking for some excitement after we get snowed in here."

The older man shook his hand, but didn't crack a smile as he climbed aboard.

As Brandon said good bye to the two of them, he noted Conrad, slipping a half eagle gold coin to the St. Louis men.

Annie seated herself at the steering oar, and her husband was amidships among the bales. Brandon and Conrad shoved off the boat and swung out the bow. One of the St. Louis men took hold of the bow line and pulled them around until the current caught both boats.

Brandon stood on the rocky shore of the island and watched with mixed emotions as the *Cincy* drew away and slowly grew smaller and smaller on the pewter-colored current of the Yukon. Just before it disappeared into a snow flurry, he saw Annie turn and raise her hand in farewell.

CHAPTER
FIFTEEN

In the camp at the bend of the river,
with its dozen saloons aglare,
Its gambling dens ariot,
its gramophones all ablare;
Crimped with the crimes of a city,
sin-ridden and bridled with lies,
In the hush of my mountained vastness,
in the flush of my midnight skies.
Robert Service

Annie O'Connell nearly screamed in panic as the boat was caught in the Yukon's current. Ignoring the tiller, she gripped the side of the boat and turned to watch the two dark figures on the island grow smaller across the widening stretch of water. It was like a knife in the heart. She had come to depend on Terry Brandon and Milton Conrad as friends, capable men she could trust to get their small party to Dawson.

But they had let her down — dumped her with no warning like unwanted, extra baggage. She swallowed the choking sensation in her throat as hot tears dimmed her vision. Brandon had said nothing about abandoning her and George to their own devices on this ice-choked river. But, she had to admit, he'd never said he was going all the way to Dawson, either. She had just assumed it. Women had the reputation of being devious, but she had always found it to be the other way around.

The panic in her heart was gradually replaced by a burning anger at these two men who had sent her on her way without so much as an hour of warning. But she should have been prepared for anything. So far on this trip, she'd discovered this was a hard country — a place where neither she nor George should be by themselves. Unlike many of the bold, assertive women she'd met along the trail, she knew her own nature to be loving and dependent. She was the type of person who would be content to lean on some strong, competent, male. When she'd married George, he seemed to be this sort. But he'd destroyed himself. The hulk of a man she saw a few feet ahead of her, huddled in his Mackinaw, was not the same man she'd known.

"There ya go, ma'am!" one of the St. Louis men in the other boat yelled across at her, shoving the bow of the *Cincy* away with an oar. "We'll stay a ways behind, keeping an eye on things in case you need any help. She's icing up pretty fast. Keep your boat in the middle of the river where the current's strongest."

"Thank you." Annie looked back at the distant island and saw one of the men waving. She raised her arm in farewell just as a snow squall swirled down and blocked them from view.

For several minutes the snow was so heavy she could barely see the bow of her boat, much less where she was in the river. She looked behind and could see nothing of the St. Louis boat. She fought down the rising panic.

182

But, as if the burst of snow were a curtain coming down on her former life, she braced herself for the next act. *Forget about the past,* she told herself. *Forget your expectations. It's all up to you now. You've got to do for yourself . . . and for George.* She pulled the fur hat down around her ears, thankful that she'd left her hair long enough to protect her neck. As the snow squall passed, she gripped the tiller and steered the boat as close to the middle of the river as she could. Ahead on the broad river she saw the dark specks of a drifting raft and a scow. The St. Louis boat was again visible, about a hundred yards to the rear. She guessed the current was running a steady five miles an hour. But even here in the middle of this wide river, large chunks of ice were scraping alongside the wooden hull. Combined with the hissing of the suspended silt, it sounded as if there were something alive in the water, gnawing at the boat.

The cold was like a heavy weight in the air, beginning to numb her fingers and toes. How long to Dawson? Brandon had said seventy-five miles. At five miles an hour, that would be about . . . fifteen hours. She could do it. She would *have* to do it. Barring any accidents, or groundings, or being frozen into the ice, she should reach Dawson sometime in the predawn hours of tomorrow morning.

Conrad had left the small iron stove in the boat. She let go of the tiller and went to fix something hot to eat. If they were to keep from freezing, she and George needed hot nourishment. It never occurred to her to ask George to do it. She had come to think of him as one would think of a helpless, aged parent who could do nothing for himself and had to be cared for like a child.

Since more than a ton of weight had been removed, the boat rode much higher in the water, and there was room to move about without climbing and crawling over sacks and bales of supplies. After kindling a fire from the small stack of driftwood left in the boat, she dug out some dried potato soup and mixed it with water in a small pot. The slushy water in her canteen was rapidly freezing so she set the big, wool-sided container near the stove. As the steam from the soup rose, so did her spirits.

When it was ready, she dipped out a porcelain mug of the mixture for George who took it without comment. She noted the dull, faraway look in his eyes. *His brain is damaged*, she thought. *He's drifted away from me.*

Soup, hot coffee, and hard crackers made the meal. She felt much better for it, and settled once again at the tiller, wrapping her feet in a blanket. The insidious cold penetrated the woolen mittens and seemed to drive the blood from her slim fingers. She pulled off one mitten at a time and tucked her bare hand inside her heavy coat and clothing, gasping at the cold fingers next to her skin. She found it the quickest and most effective way to warm numbed fingers, something she'd learned long ago during winters on the farm in Indiana. If this was only the beginning of winter in the Far North, only the prelude, what would January bring? She shivered. Perhaps Brandon was right. She and George should be in town where there was light and warmth and other people.

The long afternoon wore on with nothing to break the monotony. She stood up and moved around to stay somewhat warm. Her long woolen skirt was cumbersome. She made a mental note to change into the woolen pants she'd brought as soon as they reached Dawson. She checked on her husband.

"What're ya doin?" he demanded when she took off his shoes and felt of his toes.

"Making sure you're not getting frostbit."

"Hell, I ought to know if I'm cold. You don't have to treat me like I'm half-witted!" he grated.

That's exactly what I have to do, she thought. But aloud she said: "It's easy to get frostbite and not know it. We need to keep watching each other. If my cheeks or nose get dead white, tell me right away."

The wind gradually picked up out of the west, and, an hour later, she decided to raise the sail to increase their speed. She had assisted Conrad many times in this operation, so it was no problem for her to get the square sack sail hoisted. The increase in speed was immediate, and she could feel the pressure on the rudder as the boat snored through the water, shoving aside ice chunks and crackling new sheet ice that was forming ahead.

The St. Louis boat was being left behind, and she could see one of the men rowing hard to try to keep her in sight. Finally the men in the escort boat raised their own sail.

Dusk came on, but still Annie kept her sail drawing and her speed up. Every yard, every mile she could gain on the ice gave them a better chance of not having to walk the last few miles to Dawson. Even though she'd never experienced it, she could see the freeze-up coming quickly. The mighty Yukon would slow down and stop flowing, held rigid in the grip of the cold for the next six months.

The boat was butting and banging continuously against the solid chunks now, the ice slowing their progress. Thank God for the heaven-sent wind! If she depended solely on the current, they would never make it. How much farther? The snow clouds gradually shredded and blew away, revealing an icy-blue sky and the rapidly westering sun. She went forward, slipped the oars into their thole pins, and began rowing to aid the speed and force of the boat against the encircling ice. But, with the sail drawing and no one at the tiller, the boat yawed off course. Even if this hadn't happened, the boat was sailing faster than she could row, so she gave it up and went back to steering.

The mush ice became hard slabs until there were more ice chunks than open water. The slabs began freezing together until the boat was in the midst of one solid piece, sixty feet wide. The *Cincy* was held fast along its waterline and drifted, sometimes sideways, sometimes, stern first.

Annie let go of the tiller and went forward, loosening the halyard and dropping the sail. The ice had control of the boat now, and there was no need for sail, oars, or tiller. While George fed small pieces of wood to the

186

sheet-iron stove and huddled over it to warm himself, she dug out a short axe from their supplies. Chopping away at the new ice alongside, she worked her way around the boat. Before she could get back to where she'd started, the water had frozen again, locking them in. She dropped the axe in the bottom and sat down on a thwart, gasping with exertion. It was no use.

An hour later, with darkness almost complete, she heard a dull, grinding roar from ahead. The boat slowed and cakes of ice began to crash and smash against each other, some of them upending as they ran together. The river was jamming up. One huge slab of ice was forced atop the others and slid against the boat, crushing part of the port gunwale like the shell of a robin's egg.

"Oh, God!" Annie gasped. She grabbed an oar and tried vainly to shove the destructive ice away. A dark pool began to collect in the bottom, rising above the floorboards. But, exposed to the air, this water quickly began to solidify. Held fast by the encircling collar of ice, the boat was in no immediate danger of sinking.

Then the whole river slid to a stop. She thought it was the end of the ride. But a half hour later the Yukon heaved itself awake again and began to move. The whole river ground forward for an hour like some small glacier, scraping and groaning. She feared the boat would be crushed to kindling, but it was carried serenely along with the millions of tons of ice. Again the flow stopped. And again it started, the relentless current beneath driving the thickening ice ahead with a savage growling, grinding noise.

Just ahead, on the right-hand bank, she saw a scattering of lights. Then the river jammed to a stop one last time and went to sleep for the next six months. It had set them down almost on the doorstep of Dawson.

Annie pulled up the fur-trimmed hood of her parka and stepped out into the packed snow, closing the door softly behind her to keep from waking her husband who was snoring under the blankets in the lean-to. She walked between the buildings to the street and turned left. On reluctant feet she headed toward the Tivoli, a combination dance hall and saloon that was *the* gathering place for snow-bound Dawson. Because of the relative shortage of women in this gold boom town, she didn't expect to have any difficulty finding a job. But the thought of dancing with hairy, smelly miners, fending off pawing hands and propositions, smiling as she served them drinks made her feel queasy.

She had not worked outside the home since George O'Connell had taken her from his law office to the altar eight years ago. At thirty-five, she knew she was still attractive. It was only her state of mind and her attitude that she would have to change in order to make this venture successful. She hesitated outside the doors of the Tivoli. The place never closed, but fewer patrons were inside at nine in the morning than there would be as the day wore on.

Why had it come to this? George would be furious when he sobered up enough to realize what she was doing. But she had no alternative. He had sold their ice-bound boat and most of their supplies. With the money, he'd rented a shed built onto the back of a freight storehouse. The main attraction of the place for him was its relative cheapness, although no property in Dawson was really inexpensive. The remaining money had been used to gamble — in order to make himself a stake, he told her. Although she didn't believe him for a moment, she was almost happy because the cards kept him sober for three weeks. His luck waxed and waned. But, little by little, he finally lost most of it and had again taken to hard liquor to assuage his pain.

Only when he'd drunkenly approached her for a loan did Annie become fully aware that he'd lost or spent everything he had. It was a shock for her to find herself and her alcoholic husband nearly penniless in a boom town where gold dust was the medium of exchange and prices for staples quadruple their actual value. The greenbacks he'd flashed from his money clip during the entire trip were all he had in the world. When she questioned him, he finally admitted that he'd cleaned out his bank account before leaving home.

"Just a hundred dollars to get me into a game," he had pleaded. "I'll quit drinking until I've made us a stake . . . hell, I'll quit drinking altogether. Come spring, we'll go out and do a little prospecting, or I might take up the practice of law again. I can get a license here. There are bound to be all kinds of lawsuits over disputed claims. I'll make good money. You'll see." In the shadows thrown by the coal-oil lamp, puffy pouches under his irritated eyes looked even bigger than usual.

She had been appalled at his words, but kept her composure. "George, I don't have a hundred dollars," she had said truthfully. She had thirty-four dollars, which she was hoarding against emergencies. And this appeared to be as much an emergency as their situation was likely to produce. But she wasn't about to let him know she had any money at all. "I'm broke, too." She'd never had a poker face when lying, so she had turned away from his gaze, gathering a handful of her skirt as a hot pad to open the door of the cast-iron stove. Thrusting in a stick of wood, she had seen that it was one of the last from a dwindling pile on the floor. "Why don't you go lie down for a nap. I'll have supper ready shortly. We'll talk about it later."

He had dutifully tottered off to the pile of blankets and pillows in the corner that served as their bed on the wooden floor. She had kept her back to him as she had set about trying to find enough tinned food to make a stew of some kind. George had sold off more than half of their supplies, and they were rapidly using up the remainder. Dawson was cinching up its collective belt against increasing food shortages — even the famine that a few old-timers predicted. Some five thousand souls were cut off by winter from the outside world, dependent on their own dwindling food. There would be no supplies brought in by boat until the spring breakup. At the Tivoli, men from the creeks and local officials were even talking seriously of sending out several sourdoughs with dogsleds to bring back some emergency-relief supplies. The hopelessness of the situation had suddenly overwhelmed her, and she had had to bite her lip to keep from sobbing out loud.

That had occurred last night. Now, as she stood resolutely on the snowy Dawson street, she hoped the teeth marks on her lower lip didn't show too badly. Taking a deep breath, she opened the door to the Tivoli.

It was five o'clock on Christmas Eve when Annie slipped on her coat and left her job at the Tivoli. Owner Brice Benson had been reluctant to let her go because he was expecting a large crowd that night. But, since she was the only one of the girls who was married, he acquiesced when she begged to be allowed to go to dinner with her husband.

She hurried down the dark, snowy street toward their lean-to, excited about something for the first time in months. The snow squeaked under her shoes, and the air was like a knife to her lungs. In fact, the spirit thermometer hanging in front of the Tivoli registered twenty-eight below zero, but she was barely aware of the cold, as she anticipated their night out. It wasn't as if George had actually *promised* to take her to the best restaurant in Dawson, but at least he hadn't said no. Because of increasing food shortages, their meal would cost the standard five dollars each and would likely consist of beans, dried apples, bread, and coffee. But it was being with her husband that counted most.

Perhaps she could even persuade him to attend Mass with her in the morning at the small Catholic church on the edge of town. Or would that be pushing him too much? He professed to be a Christian, but in the time she had known him, he had attended church only on Easter Sunday and Christmas. And, since taking up John Barleycorn as a full-time companion, he'd not gone to church at all.

She opened the door to their shack, stepped inside, then stopped short with a grimace. George, who was usually a loner, sat at the tiny table with a black-haired, clean-shaven man. The visitor looked much neater than George, who now wore a gray beard two inches long.

She closed the door against the draft.

"Come in, Annie, and meet Mister Marvin Mulette," George said in more civil tones than he was accustomed to using. Probably for the sake of this visitor, she thought.

Annie looked at the dark, handsome face in the lamplight. "I've met Mister Mulette," she said shortly. "At the Tivoli, he's known as Shiv because of that big knife in his boot." She could have gone on to state that she'd been blunting his sexual advances for the past week.

Because it was a seller's market, she'd struck a deal with owner Brice Benson, that she would work at the Tivoli, but would draw the line at lowering herself to prostitution. "My dear, if my girls do that, it's strictly because they want to," the owner had said, all oily innocence. "They're on their own. I have nothing to do with it."

Now, after his continued lewd propositions, this Mulette had the gall to come here and talk to her husband. She could hardly believe it. He could have

192

had any other girl in the place for five dollars a night. Why did he insist on getting her? Forbidden fruit was always the tastiest, she realized grimly.

"How did you know where I lived?" she asked, slipping out of her parka, revealing the blue satin party dress she was required to wear on the job.

"Oh, I asked around," Mulette answered, smiling and leaning back in his chair to raise a glass of amber liquid to his lips. A bottle stood between them on the table, apparently brought by Mulette, since she knew George would never share his liquor.

"Annie, Mister Mulette has come to me with a business proposition," George said. "I know you haven't been happy in this country, and now you've had to go to work to help out . . ."

Help out? she thought. *I'm keeping us both from starving until we can get out of this god-forsaken country.* She slipped on her woolen jacket over her bare arms. It was decidedly cold in the drafty shack. He hadn't stoked the fire or chopped any more wood.

"Mister Mulette has offered me a very generous stake . . . for the privilege of escorting you out of the Yukon and back home to Cincinnati. I'll join you, of course, come spring when the riverboats begin running and . . ." He fingered a rawhide poke on the table in front of him.

"What?" Her eyes flew wide open. "My God, George, have you lost your mind entirely?" she almost screamed. She was stunned. "You're *selling* me to this slimy rodent?" Her shrill voice rang in the still air. She was quickly losing control of her emotions, but couldn't help it.

A half smile seemed frozen to Mulette's face.

"It's only for a little while, my dear, and Mister Mulette is being most generous. It's the best thing. It will help us both out of a . . . an awkward situation."

"Get out of here, you rotten excuse for a human being!" she hissed at Mulette.

No one moved for several seconds. Finally George reached under his shirt and brought out the Derringer that hung on a cord around his neck.

"Annie, I'm afraid you have no choice in the matter. I have made my decision," he said, cocking the hammer. His voice had taken on an edge, and she felt a thrill of fear up her back as she stared at the gun. "You will not make me suffer one more day. I know you have been pitying me, looking down on me as your destitute, dependent husband. And, of course, I knew it was you who dumped my supply of brandy and whisky when we were on that boat. You don't know how I suffered from the cold without that liquor!"

"No! Somebody stole it when we were portaging our supplies."

"No need to lie about it now," George said smoothly. "I won't be lacking for something to drink the rest of this cold winter. If you wish to wait for me in our home in Cincinnati, I will rejoin you as soon as I have recouped my fortunes."

"I'm not going anywhere with this man!"

"Oh, but you are. I've taken the liberty of packing most of your things. Mister Mulette owns a fine team of

194

dogs, and I'm told he's one of the best mushers in the Yukon Territory. You will make much better time going back over the mountains to Skagway than we made coming in."

She grabbed up the bottle from the table and smashed it against George's forehead. His eyes went glassy. The next thing she knew she landed hard on her back, with the wind jarred out of her. Mulette's foul breath was in her face.

The small Mulette had the strength of piano wire. She could do nothing against him as he yanked her to her feet by the front of the dress, tearing it partway off. She fought, kicking and scratching, but he retaliated by whipping the back of his hand across her face. Her nose stung and her eyes watered from the blow. She gasped, leaning both hands on the table, seeing blood drip from her nose.

"Stop fighting and I won't hurt you," he panted in her ear, gripping her arms from behind. "Get into those warm clothes. We're leaving."

Resistance was useless. The blow to her nose had taken all the fight out of her. When she realized he wasn't trying to rape her immediately, she relaxed and did as he directed, turning her back to him to step into the long, woolen underwear. She dressed in the heaviest outer clothing she possessed.

She pulled the fur cap over her dark hair, covering her ears. The mittens, tied together by a long cord, she flung around her neck. As she worked, she tried to think of a weapon that would allow her to escape. But George had the only gun, and it was on a cord around his neck. Mulette was too quick and strong for her to attempt snatching the knife out of his boot. She would wind up getting herself killed. This man didn't care. She was a plaything, something he was so obsessed with that he had paid George a lot of money for her. But if he were forced to kill her now, he'd just pick up his gold and leave, and everyone would think her husband had done it.

In five minutes she was ready for the trail. Mulette, dressed to his eyeballs in fur, grabbed her around the waist with one arm and snagged her pack with the other. The last thing she saw was her husband sitting on the floor, groggily wiping blood and whisky from his face.

Then Mulette dragged her outside into the bitter blackness of the Arctic night.

CHAPTER
SIXTEEN

**Have you known the Great White Silence,
not a snow-gemmed twig aquiver?
(Eternal truths that shame our soothing lies.)
Have you broken trail on snowshoes?
mushed your Huskies up the river,
Dared the unknown, led the way,
and clutched the prize?**
Robert Service

"How much?" Conrad leaned over the table, squinting at the tiny grains of gold that glowed warmly in the yellow light of the slush lamp.

"Hard to say. Just over a half ounce, maybe," Brandon replied, carefully sifting the small pieces of coarse gold and flakes into a square medicine bottle of clear glass they'd found in the cabin. He thrust a cork into the bottle and held it up to the light to see how much this added to the total. "Thrills me just to see something this valuable that can be dug out of the ground."

"A half ounce," Conrad said, kicking an empty box nearer the fireplace and sitting down. "That's worth about eight dollars. I can remember tipping the bellhop and the waiter at the Continental Hotel more than that in a day." He shook his head, staring into the fire. "And

197

to think how much pain, effort, and money that little bit of gold has cost us in the past four months." He snorted. "Barely enough gold in that bottle to make a watch fob."

"Can't look at it that way," Brandon replied, his jubilant mood hardly scratched by Conrad's sour words. "We've only just started. We'll have this bottle filled before Christmas."

"Not at the rate we're going," the lean man replied. "You heard what Doctor McCorkle and Jacques Musseau told us . . . that flake gold can be found all around here, but not in paying quantities."

"If we believed every rumor we've heard, we wouldn't even be here," Brandon rejoined. "Just because our neighbors on the next island want to offer their opinion, that doesn't make it true for everyone, all the time."

"Well, they got here three months ahead of us, and had several weeks of warm weather to do a lot of panning and sluicing," Conrad said, unwilling to give up the argument.

Brandon sighed and changed the subject. "First time we get to Dawson, I'm going to buy a set of small gold scales so we can really weigh this stuff."

Conrad was silent.

Brandon hoped the past four weeks of increasing darkness and cold, snowy weather was not having a negative psychological effect on his partner. "We also need to buy several dogs," he continued. "I'm getting tired of pulling that sled back and forth to Bear Creek myself."

By the time they'd moved into the cabin, winter had frozen up the Yukon and Stewart Rivers, preventing any sluicing of the river gravel. A mile and a half from the cabin, on the mainland, they'd discovered a swift spring that had remained unfrozen. The spring flowed into Bear Creek, creating several yards of open water where they dug out muck and gravel each day, hauling piles of it back to the cabin on the sled. Here it was thawed and carefully sifted with water through wire mesh into a small, canvas tank. In the past week, they'd taken to expanding their operation by building a fire of spruce to soften the frozen ground near the shore of the river, digging out the several inches of thawed sand and gravel twice a day and subjecting it to the same process. It was tedious, laborious work that had produced all too little gold, Brandon had to admit. But what else did they have to do but sit around in the small cabin, getting on each other's nerves?

"How much cash have we . . . have you . . . got left?" Conrad asked.

"What's mine is yours," Brandon corrected him. It always seemed to bother Conrad that all his money had been stolen, and, for the first time in his adult life, he was totally dependent on someone else's cash. Brandon wondered if the heir to the Conrad & Sons fortune might have a letter of credit to draw against if they ever got to a bank in Dawson.

"Oh, I don't know offhand," Brandon finally replied. "I'd have to count it. A hundred or so."

"It'll take a lot more than that to buy a decent dog team, not to mention keeping them fed."

"True enough. It was just a thought. But we've got a roof over our heads and a warm fire and enough food to last, especially since you brought down that buck last week."

The carcass had been cut into usable portions and now hung, frozen solid, high in a tree near the cabin.

"The onions are sprouting and some are rotting," Conrad said in a dull voice. "We need to stash a bag of them near the base of that far wall where they'll stay cold without freezing."

"You're right. That's the only thing we have left in our food supply that will stave off scurvy."

Even though it was mid-afternoon and the outside sky was clear, the light inside the one-room cabin was dim. The two small windows were covered with oiled paper and admitted only a little opaque light through their coating of frost. Brandon was in the process of experimenting with scraping pieces of raw deer hide to thin them, oiling them with bacon grease, and stretching them over the openings. They would be no more translucent than the paper, but considerably more durable.

The only other light was provided by a pair of slush lamps made from empty condensed milk cans filled with bacon grease, pieces of twine for wicks. The log fire in the rock fireplace was kept burning day and night for additional light as well as warmth.

The partners had been settled into their lonely existence for a month. They'd wasted no time. As soon as the boat bearing the O'Connells was out of sight, they'd set about making the cabin into their winter home. Long abandoned by some fur trapper for the Hudson Bay Company or the Alaska Commercial Company, it had taken considerable work to make it livable. Their first task was to clear the rock chimney of old birds' nests and dead leaves before chopping up windfalls and driftwood for firewood. Brandon knew they could never have too much firewood, and every spare minute was spent by one or the other of them cutting more and stacking it within easy reach of the door. Still, the voracious fireplace consumed the wood almost as fast as they could replenish it.

The first roaring fire in the hearth had made the bleak, musty cabin cheerier and more comfortable. They'd swept out twigs, pine needles, leaves, and accumulated dirt with a home-made broom, and blocked up holes chewed by rodents in the half-rotted floorboards in the corners. Then Brandon had boosted the lean Conrad up to inspect the sod-covered roof for damage. Moss had been used to chink the cracks between the logs.

A set of wooden bunks was built along one wall. The single door was at the opposite end from the fireplace, while a squat, square sheet-iron stove sat nearly in the middle of the room. The stove they used only for cooking, since neither man could ever get it to draw well.

One evening they sat playing whist and smoking in front of the fireplace that provided light and warmth for their after-supper card game. An upturned wooden box between them served as a table. The cards were water-stained but otherwise in decent condition. Sweat

201

beaded on Brandon's forehead from the heat of the fire while his feet, wrapped in heavy German woolen socks inside his trail shoes, were so cold he finally propped them up on two thick logs to get them off the floor. He puffed contentedly on his pipe, thinking he would have preferred to be reading, but the few books he'd packed had been lost in the flood at Sheep Camp.

Finally Brandon yawned and stretched. "I'm about ready for bed," he announced. "Hard work and the cold and the fact that it gets dark about two in the afternoon make me sleepy all the time." He pulled out his watch and popped open the case. "Damn! My watch stopped. I was pretty careful about keeping it wound until we got here. Guess I just got busy and let it run down." He wound the timepiece, then held it to his ear. "Ah, there it goes, but I don't know what time it is. For some reason, it bothers me not to know the time of day, or even the day of the month."

"What difference does it make?" Conrad asked. "You got some appointment to keep?"

"No, but I'd still like to know. The trappings of civilization, I guess."

Conrad removed the pipe from his teeth and set it down as he shuffled the deck together. "According to my count, it's about the Sixteenth of December, give or take a couple of days. As for the time . . . well, Wolve Saunderson and I were gamming on the ship and he told me a way he uses to figure out the time of day. I'll show you." He got up and reached for his parka. "I hope the stars are out tonight." He glanced toward the hide-covered window, as if he thought he could see through it. Frost coated the hide as well as the log walls where the moisture from their breath had frozen.

Brandon donned his parka and followed his partner outside. The air bit at his exposed cheeks. They tramped around the side of the cabin where Conrad selected a bush and snapped off two brittle, slender branches about two feet long. He trimmed them of twigs as they continued on another thirty yards toward the river, away from the trees, where there was a clear view of the night sky. So many glittering points of light speckled the black vault overhead that the sky seemed almost crowded.

"OK, let's see . . ." Conrad studied the constellations. "There's the Great Bear. Now . . . yes, there's the North Star." Lining up the North Star, he thrust the slender wands into the snow about two yards apart. "There, now. Tomorrow, the sun will be far down on the southern horizon. But when it casts the shadows of these two sticks northward in line, it will be noon and you can set your watch."

"Ingenious."

"Apparently some of these old-timers had to be the fathers of invention if they were to survive and thrive in this country."

They trooped back inside, and Brandon thrust another log into the fireplace while Conrad shed his coat, and began mixing up some batter to ferment for sourdough bread.

The next day, Brandon had the satisfaction of setting his watch by the shadows of the twigs. He slipped the

Waltham back into his pocket and looked toward the sun that was describing a low arc across the southern horizon, just above the white expanse of the Yukon River. In a few days, even the clearest sky would show only a hint of that fiery ball that gave light and life to the Earth. It would not even clear the horizon on the shortest days of the year. A strange twilight would be the only daylight they would get. The sun had gone south, leaving all of nature here in a frozen semi-death.

He shook himself out of his reverie and went to chop some fresh spruce boughs for their bunks. Besides furnishing springy mattresses, the aromatic spruce gave off a pleasant smell in the closed cabin that reeked of bacon grease and wood smoke.

The partners worked the spring at Bear Creek on one day and the fire-thawed gravel near the river on the next. Today they were hacking and shoveling the few inches of ground that their constant fire had thawed during the past few hours. By the time the gravel was shoveled onto the sled and pulled to the cabin, the pile had frozen into one hard lump and was just shoved inside the door to await a second thawing and washing.

As Brandon chopped away at the low-hanging spruce limbs, he tried to think of some way he could hold his partner for the next few months to this dreary monotony of hard labor. He would have to come up with something diverting. The entire trip from Seattle had been a wild adventure. But now this refugee from family responsibility and wealth was getting increasingly bored and restless.

Brandon had to admit that he was getting cabin fever himself, but was determined to keep at it until he had a stake large enough to invest and build on. Except for his fiancée, there was nothing for him back home. And he promised himself he would not get married unless he could afford to give her a better life, above common drudgery. He'd been a wage slave most of his life and would never go back to that. Come spring, they could pan and sluice a much greater volume of gold-bearing dirt and gravel. They could concentrate on finding gold, instead of merely surviving the weather.

He took out his frustrations by hacking savagely at the unoffending spruce. When he paused, his panting breath steamed the frigid air.

That afternoon the wind sprang up from the northwest and a leaden sky replaced the pale blue overhead.

"I smell snow," Conrad said as they dumped one last load of frozen dirt inside the cabin door.

Brandon paused from stamping snow off his boots to peer at the spirit thermometer that hung under the eave by the door. "If this thing's accurate, the temperature has gone up to eight above. A regular heat wave compared to that sixty below we had the last of November."

"Let's haul in a few more armloads of wood," Conrad said, glancing at the tall spruce trees that were beginning to moan softly in the rising wind.

Shortly after supper, snow began to fall and continued all night and into the next day. When they attempted to go outside, they found the door blocked by drifting snow.

"Damn' thing should have been made to swing inward!" Brandon muttered between clenched teeth as he struggled to force it open a few inches. They proceeded to dig their way out with mittened hands, and later with the shovel. The woodpile next to the door had acted as a drift fence and kept the blowing snow from completely blocking the south-facing door to a depth of several feet.

No work could be done that day while the blizzard continued to howl around their cabin. Conrad put in the time baking two loaves of sourdough bread, and napping, while Brandon took down his unused snowshoes from the wall and tried them on, adjusting the fastenings.

"It's within a few days of Christmas," Conrad said, two days later. "Maybe we should put up some decorations." His dull voice lacked enthusiasm.

"I've got a better idea," Brandon said, pouring himself a cup of coffee from the blackened pot on the stove. "Let's go spend Christmas in Dawson."

Conrad looked dubious. "It's seventy-five miles through deep snow."

"Hell, we need the exercise. And there are no hills. We'll pack some food and take the sled. We can travel most of the way on the river ice."

"Why take the sled?"

"I'm still looking to buy some dogs while we're there."

Conrad didn't answer.

"I think we've got enough money. If we can't afford dogs, or there are no good ones available, we could always sell the sled."

Conrad nodded.

"We've staked our claim at the spring by Bear Creek," Brandon went on. "We could record it while we're in town."

"Hardly worthwhile, considering how little gold we've got from it," Conrad said.

Brandon shrugged. "If it turned out to be something big, we'd regret not having it recorded in our names. But let's just go to Dawson for no other reason than we need some bright lights and music. I haven't seen a woman in weeks, and I know we're getting tired of looking at each other. Hell, even some bearded sourdough would look good after staring at your gap-toothed grin all this time."

"Well, if you'd let the whiskers grow out to cover that mug of yours, it would sure give *my* eyes a rest, too," Conrad said, his bearded face relaxing into a grin.

"Done!" Brandon drained his tin coffee cup and set it down. "We'll get our gear ready and start early in the morning."

CHAPTER
SEVENTEEN

**Oh, it was wild and weird and wan
and ever in camp o' nights
We would watch and watch the silver dance of
the mystic Northern Lights.**
Robert Service

"Looks like our neighbors have gone on ahead," Brandon said, indicating three dark cabins on two, low-lying islands to their left. The windows were dark and no smoke issued from their chimneys.

Conrad looked up, grunted an acknowledgement, then put his head down and continued padding a trail with his snowshoes toward the white expanse of river ahead. Brandon, hitched to the sled, followed in the flattened track.

"Nice of them to break trail for us," Brandon said when they got out onto the Yukon, where the ice was covered with several feet of snow. He pointed at a track that curved in from the left. Conrad floundered toward this new track, and they followed it on across the river, just below an ice jam where huge slabs of upended ice formed a barricade ten to twelve feet high. The trail curved north along the western edge of the river for more than two miles, and then came back out onto the snow-covered ice. The men quit talking as the exertion of walking in the unfamiliar snowshoes and pulling the partially loaded sled began to tell on them. Even the exercise of chopping firewood, along with thawing and digging in the gravel of their claims, had not been enough to keep them in as sound physical condition as when they'd arrived several weeks before.

They had set a goal of five days to reach Dawson. But, as Conrad and Brandon switched places after six miles, Brandon began to wonder if he would hold up for the nearly twenty miles they'd hoped to make the first day.

Conrad held up his hand, and they stopped to rest for five minutes, leaning against the sled, not speaking. Then Brandon helped his partner into the harness. "Ready?"

Conrad nodded, his face barely visible inside the deep hood of his parka.

Brandon turned to lead for the next several miles along the three-foot-wide track. The powdery snow was more than knee-deep on either side of the semi-packed trail. He plodded along, head down, sucking deep, steady breaths through the woolen scarf that swathed his face to the eyes. If they'd had to break trail through this virgin snowfall, they would have been lucky to make six miles in a day. He wondered what Nellie, his fiancée, would make of this hostile, frozen world. A sudden pang of loneliness gripped him. He thrust the feeling aside and concentrated on the present.

The blizzard had blown away three days before, sweeping the sky clear of clouds and allowing the temperature to plummet. Even though he'd gotten somewhat accustomed to being cold in the past two months, he'd never experienced temperatures of fifty to sixty below zero for any sustained length of time without being able to retreat indoors to a fire.

Thank God there was no wind to create a blinding whiteout that would probably be fatal. As the trail wound to the west bank of the Yukon to avoid an ice jam, then back out onto the snowfield of the frozen river, he became aware of a strange silence. He heard nothing but the sound of his harsh breathing and his own snowshoes crunching beneath him. In the dim, sunless light of midday, clumps of spruce stood silently along the riverbank, casting no shadows but showing black against the white world. In the distance, mountains humped up their white shoulders to guard the river valley.

Brandon felt a shiver of apprehension at the sight and feel of this dead, impersonal landscape devoid of other humans. Man was alien here, having no more sense than to travel abroad in such weather. Unlike the animals, man did not seek a warm den, or flee south with the sun. Humans, if they had any instinct about such things, consciously defied temperatures that sent the blood cowering back from the extremities into the trunk of the body. Cheechakos from the sunlands were braving this harsh climate for gold, the yellow metal that would give them an edge in the struggle for economic life. Brandon pictured men scrabbling for gold like predators for carrion.

The silent, empty spaces led him to reflect on the frailty of man and his place in the universe. If there was

210

a God Who created everything and held it in existence, as he'd been taught, was His indirect image to be seen in the face of this land? The rugged beauty brought to mind an image of some fierce, frost-laden, Norse god with wild hair and beard. He grinned to himself, the icy air whistling through his teeth. Surely there was only one Deity, and He also smiled on the sunlands.

The vast country around him seemed empty of any other life. But the solitude was not the overwhelming, depressing force it apparently was for Conrad. To Brandon who hated crowded, noisy cities, this was a peaceful, relaxing place where distractions didn't enter, where he had room and time to think. He idly speculated on the whereabouts of the several thousand stampeders who had crowded each other at Seattle, Dyea, Skagway, over the Chilkoot Trail, and even down the waterways with their flotilla of boats. This vast land had swallowed them up like so many ants. Were they now holed up in cabins, tents, already rotten with scurvy, or discouraged, having sold out and gone back? Who knew how many were jammed into Dawson, what number was awaiting a moderation in the weather to return by sled the way they had come? No doubt many of those hopeful Argonauts he'd seen were already dead — frozen, drowned, shot, or knifed in arguments, or had succumbed to disease and accidents, avalanches, gangrene. All — all had dispersed and gone in the space of a few weeks.

He trudged ahead, following the dim, packed trail. His moist breath, through the woolen scarf, was powdering his eyebrows white with frost. In spite of the rigors of weather and trail, he sucked in great drafts of peace, along with the cold air. Even though he had convinced Conrad to go into Dawson, he himself didn't want even to think about the milling crowds they would find there: the greed, the lying, the cheating, the drunks, the violence, the misery that civilization always seemed to bring with it, in short, fallen man at his worst where nothing — not the law of God or man — held anyone in check for long.

Brandon had always been able to endure more heat than cold, and found himself wondering if he could last through this winter without losing any fingers or toes to frostbite. By the time they paused to switch places again, Brandon was forced to pull off his mittens and thrust his hands deeply inside his armpits for several minutes to restore the feeling in his fingers. Conrad did the same, then both men removed their snowshoes to try jogging on the packed trail in an attempt to pound some circulation and tingling warmth into their numbing toes.

As Conrad resumed his place in front, he was surprised that he wasn't tired. In fact, he felt energized. Maybe it was the physical exertion of pulling the sled. Or perhaps it was the anticipation of going to town, of seeing lighted stores and saloons, of hearing a variety of voices and comparing notes with other stampeders. He would eat something he hadn't cooked himself, see sights besides the snow-bound island and the inside of their dim cabin — maybe even get a hot bath. The dullness seemed to be lifting from his mind, the weight from his feet. For the first time in weeks, he began to focus again on his purpose in coming here. It was for his wife Judith and their infant son Steven. He had to break away from Conrad & Sons and make a new life for them. The image of Judith and Steven that leaped to mind brought a pang of longing sharper than the bitter air. The baby would be crawling by now, but not yet old enough to be taking his first steps. The picture he carried of them was only in his memory, since the tiny photograph tucked inside his watch case had been lost in the flood at Sheep Camp.

A rush of anger welled up at two or three of his blood kin — his father, a maiden aunt, and a cousin — who were very likely denouncing him as an irresponsible husband who'd abandoned his duties to run off on some wild-goose chase after gold. "Lost his mind," they'd say, "when he had a fortune right at home." He sincerely hoped their denigration wouldn't turn Judith against him. She must have long since received his letter from Dyea. If he could find a post office in Dawson, he'd write her again. He felt certain the mail must be going outside by dogsled.

In the five days and four nights they spent traveling north along the frozen Yukon, the two men shook down to an economic routine of traveling and camping. Being careful to watch each other for signs of frostbite, they split the camp chores, taking turns erecting the lean-to fire-reflector, cooking, and cutting spruce boughs to place under their sleeping bags.

213

Upended slabs of ice formed a jagged, broken jam at the mouth of Sixty-Mile River. The trail crossed to the other side of the Yukon for two miles to avoid the obstruction.

"Well, you'll have to say one good thing about winter travel," Brandon said on their last night in camp as they sat between the fire and a canvas lean-to strung between two small trees.

"What's that?"

"I haven't used any mosquito netting since we started."

Conrad gave a gap-toothed grin and spat to one side, then picked up a flaming twig to relight his pipe.

Brandon told himself that his partner's morose mental state was beginning to improve.

Conrad puffed his pipe to life before gesturing over his shoulder. "That's not the only thing good about this time of year."

Brandon turned, and caught his breath. A white light was wavering up from the black horizon. As he watched, fascinated, the light seemed to flow upward, then shrink, gradually changing colors, blending from red to yellow to green, then back to white. The light expanded, flaming across the horizon, flowing like water, leaping, lighting up the sky. It was a display like nothing he'd ever seen before. The aurora borealis — the Northern lights.

"Almost makes this whole trip worthwhile, even without striking gold," Conrad murmured.

The next day, the trail skirted a mighty ice jam at the mouth of the Klondike River and led across to the east

214

side of the Yukon. In the dull mid-morning light, Brandon and Conrad trudged toward the buildings of Dawson, sprawled along the flat land at the junction of the Yukon and Klondike Rivers. Bulking overhead and dwarfing the unpainted wooden buildings was Moosehide Mountain, so called for a white scar on its flank from some ancient landslide. The landmark was visible for miles upriver.

Tired as they were, the partners didn't stop to rest until they'd taken a quick look at the winter-bound town they'd heard so much about. Front Street, the main business street, paralleled the Yukon River. Several dozen men passed up and down the street in front of rows of ramshackle buildings that housed everything from hotels to restaurants to dry goods and hardware stores. A Catholic hospital was located at the upper end of the town, while the Mounted Police barracks was at the lower end. Besides saloons, the principal business between these two ends of town were the rival Alaska Commercial Company, and the N.A.T.&T., the North American Trading and Transportation Company.

Well back of the business district was a now-frozen area of swampy land known as Hell's Half Acre, where a good portion of the red-light district was located. Yet, as they discovered that day, prostitution was, by no means, relegated to the worst parts of town.

"Saunderson mentioned there was a settlement just across the Klondike River," Brandon said, pointing.

"Officially Klondike City," Conrad said, "but known as Lousetown because the lowest caliber of whores live there."

215

Notices were posted on nearly every building for lost dogs. Other hand-lettered signs advertised outfits for sale at a dollar a pound, without flour.

Saloons, dance halls, and gambling halls appeared to be the main business of Dawson in winter. As they pulled the sled along the street, they saw the Eldorado, the Monte Carlo, the Elkhorn, and the Tivoli, all doing a lively business. Several dog sleds were moving along the snow-packed thoroughfare, bells jingling on their harnesses.

"This town doesn't even slow down to go to church on Christmas Day," Conrad remarked as they tied their sled to a porch post of the Tivoli and prepared to go inside.

"Christmas Day?" a miner exclaimed as he passed and heard the remark. "You two must have really been soaking up the hooch. Christmas Day was yesterday. You missed it."

Conrad and Brandon looked at each other, then Brandon shrugged. "Guess your mental calendar was a little off."

"Doesn't mean we can't have a drink and celebrate."

They opened the door and went inside. "Smells like steak frying," Brandon said, his stomach suddenly craving a good meal. "Let's order a bottle of wine with dinner."

While they waited for their food, Brandon stretched his legs out under the table near the front of the room. He laid aside his fur hat and parka. A wide fireplace at one end of the room blazed forth cheer and a measure of warmth into the stagnant air, adding the smell of

216

burning birch to the odor of stale tobacco smoke. A stove near the opposite end of the room contributed more heat. After being outdoors in the bitter cold for the better part of a week, Brandon felt as if he were smothering in the room.

The stool at the upright piano was empty, but from an adjoining room came the strains of a waltz dragging out of key as a gramophone wound down. Then the music stopped as someone cranked it up. Through the wide door he could see two roughly dressed miners in rawhide mukluks dancing with two girls dressed in yellow silk and red satin. A sign above the door advertised dances for one dollar each. Somewhere out of sight a roulette wheel whirred as someone tried his luck. Eight roughly clad men stood at the bar, talking and drinking.

Moose steak, beans, and sourdough bread comprised the meal. "I think this is undoubtedly the tastiest food I've ever put in my mouth," Conrad said with a sigh as he shoved away his empty plate and poured himself another glass of wine. "Everything's relative, isn't it?" he said, looking across at Brandon.

"Looks like the morning after in here," Brandon observed. "Too bad we weren't here yesterday. I'd guess they had a real blowout."

"And you'd be right," said a familiar voice from behind him.

Brandon twisted around, then jumped to his feet and gripped the hand of none other than Wolve Saunderson.

"The birth of the Lord is a time for quiet reflection and reverent prayer," said the big man. "But, hell, I'd been cooped up in that cabin with my partner for so long, I just had to blow off a little steam when I come into Dawson. Couldn't let the Cheechakos have *all* the fun. These dance hall gals think of me as their jolly old uncle, and I was doin' my best to play Santa for 'em. They were rewardin' me with free drinks. Wal, I was havin' such a good time that I took on a skinful o' hooch before I knew it. The rest o' the night's kinda hazy." He looked sheepish. "I been sleepin' it off in Benson's back room here." He rubbed a hand across his mouth and looked around. "I shore am thirsty. Think I'll have me a drink o' water and go get a hotel room and get really rested up before I go back to my claim." He looked at them. "But damn my hide, I'm goin' on about myself and I haven't even said how good it is to see both of you. You two don't look as green as you did last time I saw you at Dyea. I knew you had the makin's when I first helped you out. You look like you healed up with no permanent damage," he said to Conrad.

"Few scars on my head is all," the lean man said. "And I'm still missing my gold tooth."

"I'd ask you to have a drink with me, but I'm swearing off as of this morning," Saunderson groaned, smoothing his blond beard with one hand.

The front door flew open and a man came running in, scattering snow across the pine floor. "Where's Benson?" he cried.

"What'd you find out? Where's Annie?" A fair, red-faced man came around the end of the bar.

"Didn't see hide nor hair of her," the man said. "But you better send for Constable Barker."

"What's wrong?"

"I went around to the shack where she lives with that drunken husband and . . . ," he stopped to gasp for breath as if he'd run all the way.

"And . . . ?"

"She wasn't there, but George was . . . froze stiffer than a stick of cordwood."

"What's all this about?" Brandon asked, *sotto voce* to Saunderson.

"Girl named Annie O'Connell works here but didn't show up today. The owner sent his swamper to check on her."

"Annie O'Connell?" Brandon and Conrad exchanged startled glances. "George is dead? Damn!"

While Brice Benson sent the idle piano player down the street to the police barracks, Brandon briefly explained to Saunderson how he knew the O'Connells.

Ten minutes later, Constable Derek Barker strode into the Tivoli, stamping snow off his wolf-skin boots. "Where's this body, Benson?" he asked.

As the Mountie and Brice Benson spoke briefly, Brandon sized up the brown-haired policeman who was somewhat younger than himself. The scarlet tunic under the open sheepskin coat covered a deep-chested six-footer who radiated an air of competent authority.

Brandon, Conrad, Saunderson, Benson, and Barker were led by the swamper a block up the street and around the warehouse to the lean-to.

"I didn't touch nothin'," the man said, pointing at the shack before slipping away, apparently not wanting to look at the corpse again.

The four men crowded into the shack behind Constable Barker. The body of George O'Connell lay in a sitting position, slumped against the wall. He was hatless but fully dressed in a woolen jacket, pants, and boots. A nearly empty wine bottle was clutched in his right hand. Coagulated blood from a fresh cut formed an irregular pattern across the dead man's forehead.

Brandon tore his eyes away from the man and noticed fragments of a whisky bottle were scattered around under an overturned chair. There were frozen drops of dark blood on a corner of the wooden table. Clothes and blankets were strewn about, along with a crumpled blue satin dress. He picked it up and saw that it had an eight inch tear down the front.

"Did they fight a lot?" Barker asked, squatting by the body.

"Never, to my knowledge," Benson said.

"Looks like they got into it and she brained him with a bottle," Barker said. "Not an uncommon situation."

"This man was a drunk, and she worked to support them," Benson said. "But from everything she said and did, she loved him very much."

"Drunks can be abusive. You don't know what he was like when they were alone. Appears to me, he was drinking, and probably got mean. She was tired from working, got enough of it, and rapped him with a bottle." Barker stood up and stretched his legs. "She got scared and took off. He either froze while he was unconscious, or he came to, tapped this bottle of wine, and later passed out drunk and froze when she wasn't here to keep the fire going."

"I knew this woman," Brandon said. "I can't imagine a situation where she would strike this old man. In spite of everything, she loved him."

"From the looks of this place, they had a fight," Barker insisted. "Even the torn dress you're holding shows that."

"That's the dress she was wearing when she left work on Christmas Eve," Benson said.

"It very well could be self-defense," Barker said. "If she can be found, she'll be arrested and tried. But I'm almost certain that blow to the head didn't kill him." As he spoke, the policeman was making a more detailed examination of the cabin. "Ho, what's this?" He pulled a rawhide sack from the side pocket of the dead man's coat. He hefted the bag, then pulled open the drawstring and looked inside. "Between two and three thousand in coarse gold, I'd guess."

"I know that poke," Benson said, reaching for it. "I've held that in my safe more than once. Belongs to a man named Marvin Mulette."

"Shiv Mulette?" The constable arched his eyebrows.

"The one and only."

"Shiv Mulette was one of Soapy Smith's men who attacked you in Skagway," Saunderson said to Conrad.

Conrad nodded, his face darkening as he compressed his lips.

"I thought you said the O'Connells were destitute," Barker said to Brice Benson.

"They were," the owner of the Tivoli said. "At least, that's what she told me. And look where they're living. No self-respecting rat would live here." Benson paused, running his hand through his mop of auburn hair. "Mulette was sweet on her. Maybe he gave her this gold." He shook his head. "Funny thing is, she hated him. Couldn't stand the sight of Mulette. She complained to me several times this week that he'd wanted to take her to bed. But she wasn't a whore and told him so. But he just kept at her like he was obsessed. I had to warn him to lay off or I'd have to throw him out of my place."

"Looks like there may be more to this than I first thought," Barker said. "Shiv Mulette is wanted for various crimes, from assault to robbery. If you men will help, we'll canvass this town to see if either he or Annie O'Connell can be found. I suspect they're both long gone." He turned to Benson. "Lock up this poke in your safe for now. And ask a couple of the men at your place to haul this body inside near a stove. He'll have to be thawed some before we can straighten him out to fit into a coffin."

An hour and a half later, the quick search of Dawson had turned up nothing of Mulette or Annie. Just before he was to meet the other men back at the Tivoli, Brandon stopped to question a dog handler who also ran a kennel. The half-breed Frenchman said that a man calling himself Mulette had boarded his team at the kennel for more than a week, but had come to get them less than two days before.

222

Brandon felt himself trembling as he asked the next question. "Was he alone?"

"*Non, monsieur.* There was a woman weeth heem . . . a pretty one from the Tivoli."

"Did she say anything?"

"*Non, monsieur.*"

"Which way did they go?"

The half-breed pointed across the frozen Yukon. "Took the trail upriver."

CHAPTER
EIGHTEEN

And on we went on our woeful way,
wrapped in a daze of dream,
And the Northern Lights in the crystal nights
came forth with a mystic gleam.
They danced and they danced
the devil-dance over the naked snow;
And soft they rolled like a tide upshoaled
with a ceaseless ebb and flow.
They rippled green with a wondrous sheen,
they fluttered out like a fan;
They spread with a glaze of rose-pink rays
never yet seen of man.
Robert Service

Constable Derek Barker was skeptical when Brandon and Conrad asked to join him in pursuit of Shiv Mulette and Annie O'Connell.

"This is police business," the young, clean-shaven Mountie told them as he shrugged into his long, sheepskin coat and prepared to leave the Tivoli.

Brandon quickly explained how he'd met the O'Connells and how he and his partner had traveled downriver with them. "Since I sent the O'Connells off alone, I almost feel responsible for what happened to her," he finished.

The Mountie hesitated, wolf-skin cap in hand.

"Shiv Mulette and two of his cohorts gave me the beating of my life and robbed me of every bit of cash I had," Conrad said. He pointed at his mouth. "See this? He even knocked out my gold tooth. I'd love to get a chance at Mulette, one on one."

"I know how you feel," Barker said. "But this is not about revenge. It's about justice. The way I see it, the law is impersonal. Besides, I plan to set a fast pace and I doubt you two could keep up. On the chance that I can catch him, I don't think he's going to give up peacefully."

"I've got a rifle on our sled," Conrad said.

"We could back you, just in case," Brandon added. He eased back the tail of his woolen shirt to reveal his holstered Colt Bisley. "I'll pick up some Thirty-Eight cartridges for it."

Barker still didn't appear convinced. "Well, if you come along and can't keep the pace, I'm leaving you behind. I'm used to traveling fast and light."

Wolve Saunderson had been listening to this conversation. "I'm heading back to my cabin. These fellas may not be experienced mushers, but I am. They can travel with me. I'll make sure we all keep up, at least as far as I'm going."

"Your claim's on a creek somewhere above Sixty-Mile River, isn't it?" Barker asked.

"Right. My partner, Roger Pease, stayed there, and I came to town for Christmas." He passed a hand across his broad brow. "Whew! With the hangover I've got, I wish I had stayed there, too. You'd think at my age I'd have better sense."

"OK," Barker said, finally giving in. "Be ready to travel in thirty minutes. I'm going to hitch up my team." He turned, went out the door, and started down the street toward the police barracks.

Conrad transferred his rifle and remaining food to Saunderson's sled, and put their own sled in the care of Brice Benson for safekeeping pending their return. The shelves of the Alaska Commercial Company, a few doors away, were nearly empty of foodstuffs but were able to provide two boxes of cartridges for Brandon's Bisley.

By mid-afternoon, the brief December day was succumbing to a long Arctic night as the dark figures of four men and two dogsleds crossed the packed snow on the frozen Yukon and started upriver.

During the first two hours, Brandon discovered why Constable Barker was dubious about having company on this manhunt. He guessed the Mountie was probably five years younger than himself and in marvelous physical condition. Barker ran behind the sled most of the time, his dog whip coiled in one hand while the other rested on one of the projecting sled handles. Occasionally popping the whip over the heads of the team, he urged them to a steady, ground-eating trot, mile after mile. Now and then, on a downhill grade, he stepped up onto the back of the runners to ride for several seconds. He never looked back to see if the trio was keeping up.

Barker did not touch the animals with the whip, but used voice commands. "Let's go, Brutus. C'mon, big fella, show 'em how it's done!" he encouraged his black lead dog. "Quit lagging, Hamlet!" He popped the whip over the head of the offending animal. "Pull, Falstaff!"

Brutus, the big lead dog, was out front. The six following were hitched abreast in pairs.

The two sleds ran single-file, the Mountie in the lead, with Brandon running at his heels, followed by Saunderson's team, with Conrad riding the sled part of the time. The runners of the lightly loaded sleds hissed through the grainy snow, sliding along the single track that was grooved three feet below the surrounding snow. Brandon had eschewed his cumbersome snowshoes, preferring to jog on the packed snow with his high-topped trail shoes. He became almost hypnotized as he ran, seeing nothing ahead of him over Barker's shoulder but the bobbing, brushy tails of the seven dogs. How long could Barker keep up this pace? Brandon found himself wishing he'd gone with Saunderson, so he could at least ride the runners now and then to catch his breath. His stubborn pride had gotten him into this situation. After all, he had insisted that he and Conrad be allowed to go along on this chase. He had let it be known, with no hesitation, that he could stand the pace.

Brandon was grateful when Barker finally slowed down to spare the dogs. The only reason he was glad to be running was so he could keep his heart pumping warm blood to his extremities. Each time they slowed to walk for several minutes, he felt the bite of the extreme cold on his face and toes, and the chill of his sweat-damp skin. The illusion of slight warmth, offered by the wink of sun on the horizon at midday, was quickly gone as darkness settled in two hours later. Now the glittering, icy constellations wheeled across the heavens, promising only the bitter cold of outer space, condemning the earth to an eternal, frozen hell. Brandon thought he had experienced cold when he and Conrad traveled the five days from their cabin on Stewart River to Dawson. But, in retrospect, that seemed like springtime.

The policeman's sled was ten feet long and Saunderson's was an even dozen feet. Both sleds were of a type known as the Nome sledge, long, narrow, and light with basket-like sides. Both dog teams were fresh, and the cold air made them frisky and ready to run for the first hour, until their excess energy was burned off.

A dim whiteness was all that could be seen in the moonless night, so Brandon assumed the Mountie was trusting his team to hold the packed trail that was grooved deeply into the feathery snow.

Brandon began to think that time had stopped and eternity begun when he gradually became aware that the dogs seemed to be tiring as their pace slowed appreciably. Barker called a halt. "We'll camp here." He indicated a scattered grove of spruce, showing darker against the dim white. "Brandon, you and your partner gather as much firewood as you can carry while Saunderson and I set up camp."

Brandon gratefully retrieved the axe from the sled, and the two men set off toward a pile of dry driftwood that lay jammed against the bank of the Yukon, thrusting up at all angles from its frozen resting place. The exercise of chopping kept Brandon warm. The

228

thunking of the axe blade into the wood and the harsh breathing through a woolen scarf were the only sounds in the vast stillness. Brandon paused to pull down his scarf and, with a mittened hand, scrubbed away the clinging ice where his moist breath had frozen on the outside of the wool. The hairs inside his nostrils immediately froze, making his nose feel as if it were congested. The exposed skin of his face quickly began to lose feeling.

Now and then he could hear Conrad a few yards away, breaking off smaller dead branches. They dragged and carried the first load of wood to the campsite where the dogs had been unhitched and tethered on long leashes, far enough apart to avoid fights. Barker and Saunderson tossed half of a frozen salmon to each dog. Barker watched two of the dogs snatch the rock-hard fish with their teeth, but then lay down on the food until their warm bodies thawed the salmon sufficiently to eat it.

They positioned four heavy pieces of log on the ground next to a big rock Barker pointed out. He'd found a spot where the snow was only a foot deep in the lee of a boulder and had scraped away most of the snow covering so the fire would not melt itself into a hole.

With another axe, Saunderson was cutting birch boughs to cushion sleeping bags. A canvas fire-reflector was strung between two of the encircling trees. Soon life-saving warmth and blazing light were pushing back the cold and darkness a few feet, forming a circle of relative comfort.

Barker set about thawing hunks of beans frozen in bacon fat. Dried moose meat and bread were warmed and eaten, washed down with green spruce tea. "Best thing available to ward off scurvy," Barker remarked as Brandon sipped the bitter brew. "We could have traveled a few more miles," the Mountie added, scooping a spoonful of beans into his mouth.

Brandon couldn't imagine how he could have gone any farther.

"But I didn't want to push the dogs," Barker continued. "When the temperature is colder than fifty below, it makes for bad sledding."

Brandon looked his curiosity at him.

"The friction of the runners isn't enough to melt the tiny bit of snow that will allow the runners to slide easily. The snow crystals cling to the runners. It's like the dogs are dragging the weight of the sled through soft sand." He looked up at the glittering night sky between the tall spruce trees. "I'd guess it's every bit of sixty-five to seventy below tonight."

"Coal oil turns to slush and mercury thermometers don't work when it's this cold," Saunderson added. "The whole world begins to shut down."

Brandon pondered the frailty of the human body that would also shut down except for the narrow circle of warmth around their fire. He wondered if Mulette and Annie were spending this bitter night exposed to the elements. Were they in the same sleeping bag? He shook his head to rid his imagination of this unwanted picture, and moved closer to the fire to warm his feet. There was not the slightest movement of air. It seemed

230

as if the earth was holding its breath as it plunged into the depths of the cold.

He was startled out his reverie by a sharp, explosive crack, like a rifle shot in the darkness. Instinctively he clawed for the Colt under his parka.

"Relax," the Mountie said. "It's only the trees splitting from the cold."

Brandon took a deep breath to slow his pounding heart.

"How far did we come today?" Conrad asked, sipping the steaming tea.

"Thirty-four miles," Saunderson answered. "That about right, Constable?"

Barker nodded. "You probably know this stretch of river better than I do, since you've been traveling it a lot longer," the young Mountie said.

"How much of a lead do you think they have?" Brandon asked.

"Hard to say. They had about a forty-two-hour head start, as I figure it," Barker said. "But Mulette is probably not pushing his dogs or the woman."

"That's right," Saunderson said, "because he doesn't know anybody is after him."

"If he's taking his time, we could catch up to him in maybe a day and a half or two days."

"He might even hole up and wait out this cold snap," Saunderson said hopefully. "There are several cabins strung out at various places over the next hundred miles of river."

Brandon looked toward the dogs. Several of them were restless, turning around and around, lifting their paws gingerly, pawing at the powdery snow. Two of the Huskies were lying down, gnawing ice balls from between their toes. Looking north, he could see the aurora borealis flaming up from the horizon. The flowing brightness was white, blending into green and red, pulsing silently in the night sky like a beautiful wildfire somewhere over the edge of the Earth.

"I wonder what causes that?" Brandon asked, pointing.

"Some say it's the sun reflecting off the polar ice," Saunderson answered. "But I think it's more than that. I've never seen any kind of reflection that would waver and sink and swell and dance like that, especially in all those different colors. Some say it's electricity." He shrugged. "Nobody really knows."

The four men gazed at the show for several minutes, each man entertaining his own thoughts as he pondered the cosmic wonder of the Northern lights.

Brandon was suddenly startled by a sudden howl from one of the restless sled dogs. Several of the others began to yip and then to point their noses at the sky and give off mournful, wavering howls.

"Sounds like they've lost their last friend in the world." Conrad grinned. Then he cocked his head to one side, raising one earflap of his cap. "Listen!"

As the sled dogs' drawn-out yowls died away, an eerie, answering howling came from the distant darkness.

"Wolves," Barker said. "I thought they'd be denned up in this kind of weather."

"Well, they don't hibernate," Saunderson said. "Probably hungry. Some of the old, sick ones won't survive the winter with game scarce."

232

"I hope they don't consider us game," Conrad remarked, looking around at the darkness outside the fire circle and reaching for his Marlin on the sled.

The sled dogs again started their yipping and howling. Three of Saunderson's malamutes joined in the discordant chorus.

"My dogs do this when the Northern lights are flaring, even when there are no wolves about," Barker said. He turned to the dogs. "Shut up!" he yelled. "Portia! Hamlet! Falstaff! Shylock! Settle down."

The sobbing lament gradually died.

"Do all your dogs have Shakespearean names?" Brandon asked.

"That's what they were named when our detachment bought them. Some eccentric Englishman who bred them thought each dog had a personality that fit one of the characters in the plays."

The distant wolves gave several more wavering howls, then fell silent.

The dogs eventually burrowed into the soft snow and went to sleep, their bushy tails curled over their muzzles against the bitter air.

No one smoked a pipe after supper. Brandon stared into the flames, his eyelids growing heavy. The many miles of running, combined with the wood chopping, the hot food, and hot tea were taking their toll. His body had expended much energy just warming itself against the pervasive cold. "I'm for some sleep," he finally said, getting up and stretching and pawing for his sleeping bag on the sled.

Shortly after they'd built up the fire, each man sought his sleeping bag, while the Mountie wrapped up in a robe of rabbit skins. Each slept on a bed of spruce boughs, his feet toward the fire. Brandon loosened his stiff shoelaces and tugged off the ankle-high boots. His damp socks he propped on sticks to dry by the fire and pulled on his spare pair of German-made woolen socks. Minus only his parka, he wrapped up in the sleeping bag, drawing the hood up to form a deep cave around his face. It would not do for frostbite to affect his lungs. Before he realized it, he'd drifted into a deep, exhausted sleep.

CHAPTER
NINETEEN

They writhed like a brood of angry snakes,
hissing and sulphur pale;
Then swift they changed to a dragon vast,
lashing a cloven tail.
It seemed to us, as we gazed aloft
with an everlasting stare,
The sky was a pit of bale and dread,
and a monster reveled there.
Robert Service

"This is where I leave you," Wolve Saunderson announced at noon the next day. He came around from behind his halted sled and pulled off his mitten to shake hands with Barker and the two partners. The sourdough's steaming breath had been adding to the ice sheath on his thick blond beard all morning, and he had trouble opening his mouth to talk.

"My cabin's on Spencer Creek, about three mile up yonder way." Saunderson gestured to his right where a faint sled track led away from the main Yukon trail up along the frozen Sixty-Mile River.

"Wish you were going on with us," Conrad said.

"I know," Saunderson said, attempting a grin that cracked the ice on his beard. "Now, it's shanks' mare for you the rest of the way."

"Yeah, I'll be afoot," Conrad agreed. "But, hell, I'm mainly going to miss your company."

"I'll second that," Brandon said, taking the big man's powerful grip.

"I'd invite you up for a hot cup, and I know Pease has got something simmering on the stove. But I realize you boys are in a hurry, and we're burning daylight standing here." He slipped his mitten back on, picked up his whip, and walked around to the rear of his sled.

Constable Barker had been restlessly shifting his weight and glancing at the low hills upriver where the invisible sun was still below the horizon. The blaze of noon sun shone somewhere far to the south, over the curve of the earth. Here, it cast only a gray pall in the clear sky.

Then something caught the Mountie's eye, and he moved to where the faint, trodden sled trail curved off to the west. Head down, he snowshoed through the white powder, carefully examining the track for a stretch of some thirty yards. The three other men watched him stop and stare off toward a copse of trees where the track disappeared.

"Do you think your partner might have come down this trail since you left for Dawson?" Barker asked.

"No."

"How can you be so sure?"

"I partnered up with Pease ten years ago. And I've spent more time with him than any other human. I know him. He hates this kind of weather. I'd wager he hasn't set foot outside our cabin since I left, unless it's just to get some hunks of stove wood off the pile by the door."

Barker nodded thoughtfully, and looked up the side trail again.

"Why do you ask?"

"Another sled has gone over this trail since you came out. Now that I look at it again, I can see where the snow-shoe tracks lead *toward* your cabin, not away from it."

The three men waited for him to continue.

"I think we should follow this trail. There aren't many men out in weather like this. It could be the one we're after. He might have gone up your back trail looking for shelter."

"How long ago do you think?" Saunderson asked.

"Hard to say. There has been no wind for the past four days, so the indentations haven't been sifted in. The tracks are still sharp. It may just be some musher headed up Sixty-Mile back to his claim who decided to travel in the tracks you'd already made. We don't know for sure that Mulette is headed directly out of the country." He walked back to his sled. "We'll travel with you back to your cabin and ask your partner if he's seen anyone in the past few days. It's only three miles out of our way."

In the softer snow of the partially packed side trail, it took them three quarters of an hour to reach the cabin.

"Funny," Saunderson said, halting his team out front. "No smoke comin' from the chimney."

Barker slipped off his right mitten as he reached for a rifle. He worked the lever of the Winchester, the ratcheting noise ripping the still air.

Taking a cue from the lawman, Conrad slid his Marlin out of the dunnage on the sled, and Brandon pulled his Colt from under his parka.

The Mountie reached down and loosed the rawhide ties on his snowshoes. The three men fanned out as Saunderson approached the solid plank door. There was only one window in the front wall of the cabin, and it was covered with some sort of opaque material.

Saunderson silently held up his hand for the others to desist while he approached the door and took hold of the latchstring. Yanking up on the rawhide, he shoved the door inward with a booted foot. "Yo, Roger! I'm back!" he shouted, stepping quickly aside. The door swung inward with a creaking sound. The open doorway gaped at them, black and silent.

Barker motioned with his head, and Brandon nodded that he understood.

"Now!" Barker darted inside and to the left. Brandon, right on his heels, sprang in to the right, to avoid being silhouetted in the doorway. Temporarily blind in the dim interior, Brandon gripped his Colt. He crouched, his heart pounding, praying no gunshots would flash out of the dark before he could see. He held his breath for the space of several heartbeats. Finally, as his eyes adjusted to the dimness, he let out a long breath and straightened up. The cabin was empty. He let down the hammer of his Colt and holstered it.

"All clear!" Barker called to the men outside.

"Oh, my God! Roger!" Saunderson sprang across the room.

Brandon saw a pair of legs encased in caribou mukluks on the floor behind the table. He cast a sharp glance at the Mountie, as the four men crouched beside the body of Saunderson's partner. The big man was biting his lip to hold back the tears.

"Shot at least twice with a big-bore weapon," Barker said. Getting to his feet, he crossed the room and opened the stove door. He held a hand inside, then tentatively pushed his fingers into the ashes. "Still warm. The killer hasn't been gone from here more than eight or ten hours. Probably early this morning." He turned to Conrad. "Get a fire going."

For the first time, Brandon noticed it was nearly as cold in the room as it was outside, but it was a clammy chill that made him shiver. While Conrad was finding matches and kindling, Brandon examined the body of Roger Pease. The dead man lay on his back, rigid. Iced blood stiffened the front of his plaid shirt, and a frozen trickle from the hole in his forehead left no doubt about the cause of death. His glazed eyes were wide open, and he had a startled look on his bearded face. By his right hand lay a frying pan containing congealed grease. Three tin plates with remnants of food on them, along with cups and forks, littered the table.

"Surprised in the act of hospitality," Barker muttered, looking down at the body. He went over to Saunderson who sat on a stool, head in his hands. "I know this is hard for you, but do you have any idea who might have done this? Somebody Pease knew? Can you look around and tell me if anything is missing?"

239

Saunderson straightened up with a groan. "Roger Pease had his odd ways, like most people, but he never made enemies." With an obvious effort, the big man got up as if the weight of his body was more than his legs would bear. He looked stunned, distracted. "There," he finally said, indicating an iron ring set in the plank floor. "We kept a bearskin rug over that."

Barker gripped the ring and heaved open the two-square-foot trapdoor. "What's under here?"

Saunderson dropped to his hands and knees to inspect the space under the floor. "Nothing now. Damn! Not this, too! Somebody got it all!" He slammed the flat of his hand on the floor.

"What?" Barker asked.

"All the rawhide pokes of coarse gold and flour gold . . . all the dust we'd washed and dug out for ten years. Amounted to about a hundred and sixty thousand."

Brandon gave a low whistle.

"Poor Roger. What did it get him?" Saunderson muttered, rocking back from his knees to a crouch and staring at his partner's body. "All the struggle and the frostbite, and the eating of bacon and beans for years so he could go out to the States a rich man? Some damn' thief and murderer came and took it all."

Conrad left the stove door open, and the blaze was beginning to force the damp chill into the corners of the room.

Barker was examining the one-room cabin with the aid of a coal-oil lamp. "Did Pease have any weapons?"

"A rifle that was hanging on that set of antlers on the wall," Saunderson said. "I see it's gone, too." He rummaged in a wooden box on the floor. "And the rotten skunk got the extra ammunition that was in here."

"What's this?" Barker picked up something tiny from the floor. He held the smoky lamp up to it. "Looks like a little gold pin of some kind."

Brandon peered closely at the object, and his heart leaped. "The initials AMH . . . Anna Marie Hosher."

"Who's that?" Barker asked.

"Annie O'Connell's grandmother. The woman she was named for. Annie showed me that pin one evening in camp on the river."

Barker took another look, then shoved the pin into his pocket, and let out a long breath. "It looks like Mulette is now wanted for murder and robbery, along with kidnapping and assault. Stay here and take care of your partner," Barker said, striding toward the door and ripping a piece of sourdough bread from the loaf on the table as he went. "If you boys feel up to a real run, we might be able to catch him. We've got at least two hours of decent daylight left. Mulette didn't go out the same way he came in, so he's left a fresh track somewhere leading away from here." The Mountie picked up his rifle leaning against the wall, then paused at the door and turned back to Saunderson. "Do you have any extra salmon for my dogs?"

The big man went outside to the cache at the back of the cabin. "Damn! The fish is gone. He thought of everything. I even had twenty pounds of salmon eggs, and he took them, too."

"Not surprised," Barker said. He knows that somebody will be on his trail sooner or later, and he'll be moving fast now. He won't want to be slowed down by having to find food for his team." He gnawed thoughtfully at the bread. "They likely rested here last night. Now they have several hours' head start." He shook his head ruefully. "And Mulette knows how to get the best from his dogs."

"We were lucky Annie had the good sense to drop that little pin and leave us a clue," Brandon said.

"And luckier, still, that you recognized who it belonged to," Conrad added.

Saunderson came to the door of the cabin. "Constable, you're welcome to any of my dogs you think are stronger or in better condition."

Barker hesitated, looking over the resting team that was still harnessed to Saunderson's sled. "Good idea. I'll pay you for them. My harness is only made for seven, but I'll take two of yours for replacements, just in case. How about that gray one and the one with the reddish coat?"

"Boots and Nooka. Good choice." While the two men were unhitching the dogs, Saunderson said: "You know, Mulette may not be traveling as fast as you think."

"Why's that?"

"A hundred and sixty thousand in gold weighs over six hundred pounds."

"And if Annie is riding the sled part of the time, she weighs at least a hundred and thirty," Brandon added.

242

"All that's in our favor," Barker said. "But a good, strong dog team can pull a thousand-pound load at four or five miles an hour on level ground for thirty miles or more. With all their food and gear, they probably don't exceed a half ton." He nodded to Saunderson as he secured the two new dogs on long tethers behind his own sled. "But you're right . . . every little bit will help." He straightened up. "I'll give you an I.O.U. for the dogs if you don't need the cash until I get back."

Saunderson shrugged. "I just lost a hundred and sixty thousand. What do I need with a few dollars? I'm not going anywhere. I'll wrap up poor Roger and lay him out in the lean-to. Can't bury him till spring anyhow."

"All right." Barker pulled a small notebook from his inside coat pocket and, with a short pencil, scribbled something, tore out the page, and handed it to Saunderson. "See you on the way back." He turned to Brandon and Conrad. "Better get those snowshoes on."

They picked up the trail of Mulette's sled quickly. It led away in a southwesterly direction from the side of the cabin, wound down along the creekbank for more than a mile before crossing the frozen Sixty Mile River. Barker led the way, further tramping down the feathery snow to ease the passage for the dogs and sled behind him.

An hour later, the Mountie halted the team on the crest of a low hill and walked back to them, breathing heavily. "This will slow him even more than his six hundred pounds of gold," Barker commented.

"What will?" Conrad asked.

"He's breaking trail through three feet of virgin snow for his own team," he panted. "If he's making one to two miles an hour, he's doing well . . ." His warm breath formed a steamy halo around his head. "But he can't keep up that pace for long. And the woman won't be any help to him." He smiled grimly, his face flushed pink from the cold and exertion. "If you think it's hard going for us, imagine what he's dealing with. As long as he stays off the main Yukon trail, the quicker we should be able to overtake him." He paused to breathe deeply through his nose.

Brandon pulled the woolen scarf away from his own face. Either he was being warmed by the exercise, or the weather was moderating. He glanced at the sky. A thin overcast was sliding up from the southwest on some unfelt wind high aloft, like a gray cosmic blanket being pulled over their white world. He clamped his hands under his armpits and pulled off his mittens. The air temperature was probably no more than twenty-five or thirty below zero.

Five minutes later, they moved out again, this time with Brandon leading the way. After a half hour of this toil he began to appreciate fully the stamina and endurance of the Mountie. The webbed frames under his feet gave the snow a light, feathery feel. But moving quickly to keep ahead of the eager dog team was another matter. He had to walk with his feet slightly apart to avoid stepping on his own snowshoes, and he

244

discovered quickly that he could not slide or shuffle his feet without catching the upturned ends of the snowshoes, and stumbling. Every step had to be deliberate. It required that he lift his leg, swing it forward, and set it down, further compacting the partially broken trail. Up, forward, down. Up, forward, down. Get into a rhythm. Twenty yards, fifty yards. Lungs burning, thigh muscles aching, perspiration dampening his inner clothing. Look ahead. Block out the pain. Concentrate on making it to where the faint trail bent around that clump of spruce ahead.

The grueling effort finally broke his will, and he made up his mind to stop. Just a few more steps . . .

"Hold up a minute!" Barker called, saving Brandon's pride. Brandon halted in his tracks, head down, legs trembling, laboring to suck great drafts of thin, bitter air through his open mouth. Better to die later of frostbite of the lung tissue than to pass out from asphyxiation or drop from a heart attack.

"We're losing the light," the Mountie said. "Mulette was probably traveling this stretch with nothing but starlight and maybe a pocket compass to guide him." He looked around as if to get his directional bearings. "I think he's finally angling back toward the main Yukon trail."

Thank God, Brandon thought.

"Let Conrad lead for a while."

They exchanged places, and Brandon fell back to bring up the rear behind the two tethered dogs.

An hour after gray day had turned to early dark, they stumbled out of the heavy snow onto the main trail along the broad, white surface of the sleeping Yukon. The dogs had no trouble following the packed trail, and for several hours all Brandon heard was their breathing and the hissing of the sled runners through the dry snow.

Nine hours after leaving Saunderson's cabin, Constable Barker called a halt. "These dogs are about done in," he explained, as if by way of apology for not going on. Brandon was numb with fatigue and cold. They hadn't stopped now for food and rest for themselves, but because they risked losing one or more of their dogs.

Moving automatically, Brandon didn't allow himself to stop until he'd helped chop firewood and set up camp behind a copse of trees along the riverbank. Barker unhitched the team, pitching half a salmon to each of the dogs. Conrad handled the cooking chores, which consisted of making tea and thawing out the leftover beans, bacon, and bread.

An hour later, warmed by a roaring blaze and filled with food and hot tea, Brandon began to feel a little life sleeping back into his body. It was fortunate the food and fire were performing their restorative work because Barker said: "We'll rest the dogs, and ourselves, for four hours . . . no more . . . then we'll take the trail again.

Brandon threw a glance at Conrad who was sitting across the fire from him. The red-rimmed eyes narrowed and the bearded lips set in a grim line. But Conrad said nothing; he, too, had agreed to follow the directions of this experienced policeman. Brandon guessed his partner had never been physically or mentally tested as he was being tested now.

"We must have made up a lot of time on Mulette today," Barker went on, giving no indication of the fatigue he must have been feeling as well. "We have to be tougher than he is. He's burdened by the gold and the woman and the deep snow. He might think no one will know who committed that murder and robbery, but he'll still get out of the country as fast as he can in case the law does come after him." He looked up at Brandon with blue eyes that were unusually bright in the firelight. Brandon saw, in that square-jawed face, not the efficient, stable policeman, but a manhunter, driven by an obsession. "There's no way he can know anyone is this close on his trail," Barker said. "We have to follow up our advantage."

Brandon nodded. "I'm ready." It was an outright lie, but it was the only thing he could say.

"Hamlet is coughing a little blood, and Falstaff is limping. I'll have to replace one or both of them with Saunderson's dogs. That'll help some," the young Mountie murmured as he stared into the flames.

"How are we going to wake up in four hours?" Brandon asked, his eyelids growing heavy.

"I'll set my mental alarm clock," Barker replied. "Works every time."

Brandon was too tired even to think how unlikely this assertion sounded. "Wake me when you're ready," he said, loosening the stiff rawhide laces on his trail shoes. His pride had carried him most of the way this day, but now he didn't care who put the last wood on the fire, or that he had no spruce boughs under his sleeping bag. He simply crawled inside, making sure he was not too close to the fire, and passed out.

CHAPTER
TWENTY

And the skies of night were alive with light,
with a throbbing, thrilling flame;
Amber and rose and violet,
opal and gold it came.
It swept the sky like a giant scythe,
it quivered back to a wedge;
Argently bright, it cleft the night
with a wavy, golden edge.
Pennants of silver waved and streamed,
lazy banners unfurled;
Sudden splendors of sabres gleamed,
lightning javelins were hurled.
Robert Service

It seemed to Brandon he had just closed his eyes when a hand was shaking his shoulder. "Huh?"

"Time to go," came Barker's voice from somewhere.

Brandon struggled up from the dark pit of oblivion. With a groan, he managed to escape from the sleeping bag, his stiffened body protesting every move. Pushing to his feet in the bitter air, he slipped into his knee-length parka, throwing the fur-lined hood over his matted hair.

Barker had the fire stirred up and was heating some left-over tea. He'd set their canteens to thaw near the blaze. Suddenly very thirsty, Brandon took a long drink from his two-quart, blanket-sided canteen, rinsing the foul taste from his mouth. Then he scooped a handful of snow, melted it in his hand, and washed his face with the cold water. He repeated the process, feeling the puffiness in his gritty eyes and the stubble on his cheeks.

Stepping away a few yards into the darkness, he urinated in the snow. It must be between two and three in the morning, he guessed. The high, thin clouds had passed away, leaving the heavens spangled with millions of glittering ice chips. He stared in fascination at the Northern lights that were performing their writhing, sinuous dance, leaping and lancing above the horizon.

Back at the fire, Barker handed him something. "Pemmican," he said. "You can go a long way on that."

Brandon gnawed at the fist-size chunk of food. Without looking, he knew it was composed of pounded berries and shredded moose meat congealed with animal fat. Not especially tasty, but he'd recently come to think of food as fuel, rather than as a pleasure for the palate. The Mountie handed him a cup of hot tea to wash down the quick breakfast.

A deep growl was followed quickly by snarling and snapping and the thrashing of bodies. "Ha! Break it up, damn your hides!" Barker sprang away with a hunk of firewood to separate the fighting dogs. The sound of a club thudding into bodies. Yipping and yelping in the dark as the animals were beaten away from one another. "Save that energy for the trail," Barker said, yanking the dogs, one at a time, to the harness.

Shortly, Barker was lashing the last of their gear on the sled as Conrad kicked snow over the hissing fire. Barker rocked the sled to break the runners loose from the frozen ground, then popped his whip over the team, and they were off. As Brandon jogged along behind Conrad and Barker, he began to feel better. The warmth was flowing back into his aching muscles as he settled into the rhythm of the pace.

Some three hours later, Barker drew the team to a halt and strode to a dark lump in the snow just off the trail. "A dog," he said, striking a match to get a look at the dead animal. "Shot in the head. Must've gone lame." The match flamed out, and he stood up. "Very likely one of Mulette's dogs." He reached for his belted knife under the heavy coat, then stooped to slit the belly of the carcass, sliding his bare hand inside. "Still a little warm. He's not far ahead." He wiped his hand and the blade in the snow and stood up. "This will give me a chance to drop off Hamlet."

The dogs whined, moving around in the traces as they smelled the nearness of death. Barker worked in the darkness to unhitch the wheel-dog. "Good boy! You gave it all you had. Here's a piece of fish. And, if you don't mind eating your own, there's some fresh meat for you."

He hitched Boots, one of Saunderson's trailing dogs, into harness. Did the Mountie think Hamlet could survive on his own, possibly with a frostbitten lung? Or did Barker not want to risk the noise of a gunshot?

"Hyah! Mush, Brutus!" The whip cracked in the darkness, and the sled was hissing along the trail again.

It was an hour after daylight when they came around a curve in the trail and spotted the dark outline of a sled a quarter mile ahead. Brandon's heart began to pound at the sight of their quarry.

"Is it Mulette?" Conrad panted.

"Likely," Barker replied. "Damn! I was hoping to catch him in camp."

Gray daylight showed the sled was following the trail where it led down the bank and out onto the snow of the frozen river.

"Make sure your weapons aren't froze up," Barker said. "Looks like it's going to be a dash to the finish."

Brandon unbuttoned the parka so his Colt would be ready to hand. Barker drew the team to a halt and reached for his Winchester in its sheath under the sleeping bags. He checked the load, as Conrad was retrieving his Marlin.

"If this is our man, I don't want any shooting unless I give the word," Barker said, replacing the rifle. "We'll take him alive, if possible. And I don't want this woman hurt."

Etched sharply against the white background, the dog team up ahead was pulling the sled at a walk.

"Ready?"

They nodded.

"Hyah! Mush!" The Mountie popped his whip over the heads of the dogs. "Up, Brutus! Boots! Portia, pull!"

252

The three men ran behind the bouncing, yawing sled for seventy yards before the driver ahead looked back and saw them. He immediately turned and lashed his dogs to a run.

But his team had little left. The gap began to close quickly. They drew closer and closer along the one-track trail. There was nowhere to seek cover on the flat river. Brandon saw the white face of a woman on the sled, looking back at them. The driver was riding a runner with one foot and pushing with the other as he yelled at his team and lashed them unmercifully with his whip. He looked back over his shoulder.

"That's Mulette," the Mountie said. "I'd never forget that face."

As the gap closed to fifty yards, Mulette suddenly leaped for the gee pole and threw his weight against it. The sled slewed sideways and tipped over, throwing the woman out, while the team, caught by surprise, floundered in the tangled harness.

"Look out!" Barker yelled as Mulette jumped behind the overturned sled, bringing a rifle to bear.

Two quick shots shattered the stillness as Brandon and Conrad plowed, face down, into the snow alongside the trail. Brandon gasped as the freezing powder went down his neck and up his sleeves. He rolled over and struggled to yank off his mittens and get at his holstered Colt.

More shots exploded as Barker and Conrad returned fire, but the muzzle blasts sounded more like firecrackers as most of the noise was swallowed up by the vast stillness around them. Two of their dogs were hit and dropped. The others, sensing this new danger, were leaping against the restraining harness. Nooka, Saunderson's one remaining dog on a lead string, broke his tether behind the sled and lunged away through the snow.

Brandon brought his Colt Bisley up and got off three shots, then winced as a slug splintered the handle of the sled near his head. The acrid smell of spent gunpowder filled the still air.

Using the sled for cover, Barker and Conrad fired at the dark, hooded figure. Off to the left of the sled, the woman was trying to crawl away through the deep snow. Mulette sprang out from his cover to grab her just as one of Barker's slugs found its mark. Mulette lurched sideways, but still managed to grab Annie around the neck with one arm and use her as a shield to worm his way back to the shelter of his sled.

Barker put a hand on Conrad's arm for him to stop shooting. Several seconds of silence followed. "Give it up, Mulette! This is Constable Derek Barker of the Mounted Police. You're under arrest!"

There was no reply.

"You're hit!" Barker shouted. "There's no place to go."

"I've had infected mosquito bites worse than this!" came Mulette's booming answer. "Now, I'll give the orders. I've got my blade on her throat. I've had my fill of her for a few days. You'll do as I say, or she'll be meat for the wolves."

"We know you murdered Roger Pease and stole that gold! You'll never get out of this country alive."

254

"If I don't, you don't!" Mulette yelled.

"We're three against one. Better give it up and take your chances in court!" Barker shouted, keeping his head down behind the loaded sled.

"Here's one reason why I'm in charge!" Mulette yelled. Several seconds of silence passed while he scrabbled around. Then he heaved a stick in a high arc toward them. Just as it touched the snow midway between the sleds, it exploded with a roar, throwing a shower into the air. The dogs yelped and leaped, trying to escape. Brandon stared at a blackened, gaping hole in the snow and, through the ringing in his ears, heard a laugh from across the space between them.

"Dynamite!" Barker groaned. "Damn! Saunderson didn't mention missing any of that."

"Now, you will throw out your weapons and walk over here!" came Mulette's triumphant shout. "Then we'll combine the best dogs of our teams, and I'll be on my way. If you co-operate, I'll let you live. Maybe you can walk out of here . . . without any food."

"He's wounded," Brandon said. "He can't throw a lighted stick of dynamite almost fifty yards . . . let alone, time the fuse so it goes off before the snow can snuff it out." He looked at the Mountie. "We could wait him out. Or I could go for help." Even as he said it, Brandon knew both suggestions were impractical.

Barker was silent for a moment. "He just said he needs our remaining dogs. If he blew us up, he'd kill the dogs, too. Then he'd have to camp and rest his own team before he could go on. He can't haul that gold by himself, and he's not about to leave it."

"Looks like a stand-off," Brandon said.

"Let me try a shot at him," Conrad whispered hoarsely.

"No. You might hit the woman."

Conrad raised his eyes above the edge of the sled. "Constable, I've got ribbons at home for marksmanship. Shooting matches were a favorite sport of the idle rich when I was growing up. I know I can clip him, without hitting Annie. This Marlin is dead accurate, and my target's only about fifty yards away, silhouetted by a white background. She's not big enough for him to completely hide behind. Let me try it."

The Mountie hesitated, struggling to figure out another way. Finally he said: "You have one chance. If your aim is off only a few inches, you could kill her. If you just wing him, he'll kill her. Or you could hit the dynamite and there wouldn't be enough left of them to bury."

Conrad nodded his understanding of what was at stake.

"I'm waiting for your answer!" came the gloating shout from Mulette.

"We're discussing it!" Barker yelled back. "Give us a minute."

"You have sixty seconds by my watch, starting now!"

While this exchange was taking place, Brandon saw Conrad take a deep breath to steady himself, then ease the barrel of his rifle up over the load on the sled. The sled was still twitching as the dogs jerked in the traces, trying to get loose. The lean, bearded man paused for several seconds until the animals settled down. Then he

256

slid back the hood of his parka, laid his cheek against the polished walnut stock, and sighted slowly, deliberately.

Brandon stared at the distant figures of Annie and Mulette. He could feel his heart thudding in his chest — four beats, five . . . six . . . The Marlin jumped and roared, and Mulette flung up his arms, rifle spinning backward over his head.

The three men were up and running before Mulette's rifle hit the snow. Annie was scrambling away on her hands and knees. Mulette lay on his back with his eyes shut, but Brandon couldn't see where he'd been hit. Barker picked up the shattered rifle, showing that Conrad's slug had smashed the receiver and apparently thrown the weapon back into Mulette's head, knocking him unconscious. A purpling bruise was forming on the man's forehead.

"Annie, are you hurt?" Brandon sprang to the woman's side, helping her up from the snow. She shook her head, brushing the disheveled hair away from her face.

Barker flung the mangled rifle away. "Let's get him lashed to this sled and then make camp to get sorted out. We'll hitch these sleds in tandem. If we rest until tomorrow, the dogs we've got left should be able to haul us back." He looked around thoughtfully, all business. "We'll leave the dynamite here, and drop the gold with Saunderson." He turned toward Conrad. "That was a great shot."

"I wasn't aiming for his rifle."

"Better than a kill shot, anyway," Barker replied. "I didn't bring any manacles with me. That rope on our sled we use for the lean-to . . . get it so we can tie this man."

Brandon was hugging Annie. Over her shoulder he caught a movement out of the corner of his eye. "Look out!" he shouted, flinging her aside and yanking his Colt. Mulette lunged toward Barker. The foot-long blade of a Bowie knife ripped into the Mountie's back. Brandon's Colt exploded, and Mulette pitched sideways into the sled.

Conrad kicked the limp form of Mulette over as Brandon and Annie leaped to Barker. The bone handle of the knife still protruded from the thick sheepskin coat.

"I think I'm OK," Barker gasped. He stripped off the coat. The red tunic underneath was ripped from the shoulder down to the armpit, and blood was soaking the scarlet cloth another shade of red.

"The blade slid right down between your body and your left arm," Brandon said, when they got the tunic off. "A pretty good gash, but the cold should stop the bleeding fairly quick. That thick sheepskin coat probably saved you any further damage."

"What about M . . . Mulette?" Barker asked, his teeth chattering in the frigid air.

"Dead," Conrad said, pressing two fingers to the carotid artery.

"I'd hoped to bring him in alive," Barker said, grimacing as Brandon packed a handful of snow against the wound, through the slit in his white long johns.

258

"Saved the government the expense of a trial and hanging," Conrad said.

"What a nightmare!" Annie sobbed. Brandon could feel her trembling as she clung to him.

"Then it's about time to start waking up," he said, kissing her on the forehead.

CHAPTER
TWENTY-ONE

They rolled around with a soundless sound
like softly bruised silk;
They poured into the bowl of the sky
with the gentle flow of milk.
In eager, pulsing violet their
wheeling chariots came,
Or they poised above the Polar rim like a coronal
of flame.
Robert Service

"Are you going Outside as soon as the spring breakup comes?" Terry Brandon asked Annie O'Connell three weeks later as they sat in the Tivoli. He had to raise his voice to make himself heard over the party that was in progress. The whir of a roulette wheel and the rattle of dice blended with loud voices, laughter, and the clinking of glassware. About twenty feet from the glowing potbelly stove, a perspiring piano player was pounding out a tinkling ragtime melody.

Wolve Saunderson and Milton Conrad sat at the table with them, while Brice Benson, the Tivoli's proprietor, stood looking on. Overhead coal-oil chandeliers, along with a roaring blaze on the hearth, held the Arctic night at bay and imparted a bright, festive glow to the big room.

260

"Spring is five months off yet," Annie answered. "I'll have to wait and see. Plenty of time for me to make up my mind whether to leave or stay. Meanwhile, Mister Saunderson . . ."

"Wolve," he corrected.

"Wolve got me a job working with Nellie Cashman at her new boarding house here in town."

"With the money you've got, you don't need to work," Brandon said.

"It's good to occupy my mind," she said. "I still think Mister Sau . . . Wolve should not have given me that gold. I didn't do anything to deserve it."

The big sourdough's ruddy complexion deepened in the lamplight, as all eyes at the table turned toward him. "Roger Pease didn't live to spend it," he rumbled in a deep voice. "And he had no kin that I know of. I'm sure he would have wanted me to split it with the folks who took care of his murderer. After all, eighty thousand split three ways with you and Conrad and Brandon only comes to a little over twenty-six thousand apiece." He upended his tin mug of beer.

Brice Benson took the empty mug from his hand and signaled one of his bartenders. "All the drinks for this group are on me tonight," he said. "I just wish Constable Barker had been able to join us."

Brandon turned to Conrad. "What are you going to do now?" His partner had been unusually quiet.

"This experience has taught me that I can do damn' near anything I set my mind to," he replied slowly. "If that flake gold is actually found in small quantities spread over a large area, I'm thinking of having a floating dredge built that will work up and down the rivers, sifting tons and tons of sand and earth and filter out the gold in paying quantities. If my twenty-six thousand won't pay for a machine like that, I might be able to persuade our company board of directors to finance it as an investment."

"So you've decided to take over your family business when you hit thirty?" Brandon asked.

"I'm going home and take one more close look at it, but I've pretty much made up my mind to abdicate in favor of my younger brother. This North country is beginning to grow on me. I want to bring my wife and son back up here and live for a time while I supervise this dredging operation I have in mind."

Brandon eyed his partner. No longer the well-groomed city boy, Conrad sported a thick black beard and hair to his collar. With rest and food, his rheumy, red-rimmed eyes had cleared up, but the skin over both cheek bones was still a mass of blackened scabs where the frost had bitten. The missing gold tooth now hung around his neck on a cord. It had been retrieved from Mulette's pocket.

"Since Roger's gone, I'm pretty much at loose ends. I'd be obliged for some company at my cabin now and then," Wolve Saunderson said. "Beautiful, female company wouldn't be sneered at, neither." He looked at Annie as he spoke.

The blush gave her skin a healthy glow. She gestured toward the adjoining room where a gramophone had begun to blare and several couples were whirling to the music. "Wolve, I don't work here any more, so it wouldn't cost you a dollar to dance with me," she said with a smile.

The world should be full of people like these two, Brandon thought as he watched the big sourdough escort Annie toward the dance floor in the next room.

He leaned back in his chair with a contented sigh. A good, steamy bath and shave, a haircut, and a change of clothing at Nellie Cashman's boarding house had made a new man of him. Actually it was this trek North that had made a new man of him, he reflected. He'd never in his life felt more confident about himself and the future. Except for the cracked and peeling skin on his lips and hands from the frost, he was also in the best physical condition of his life. In spite of a diet heavy in starch and fat, the onions and the green spruce tea had kept scurvy at bay.

Brandon fingered the rawhide poke on the table in front of him. It contained only a few hundred dollars in coarse gold — a tiny fraction of his more than twenty-six thousand share. The remainder was in Benson's safe. He was certain that with a few wise investments — possibly even in Conrad's gold dredge — he could parlay his stake into a reasonable fortune. Careful management of his money would keep him from ever being a wage slave again.

"Thinking of your family?" Brandon asked, interrupting his partner's thoughtful silence.

"Yeah," Conrad admitted. "Wish they were here to spend the rest of the winter with me."

"As much as they miss you, they'd probably rather be in Baltimore," Brandon said soberly.

"Why do you say that?"

"Because you can lay odds it's not forty below there tonight."

Conrad gave him a gap-toothed grin. "And it's highly unlikely your fiancée, Nellie, is watching the Northern lights over the frozen Ohio River."

"Here's to absent wives and girl friends!"

Their tin mugs clashed in a toast.